Mia

a

matter

of

taste

SIMON SPOTLIGHT

An imprint of Simon & Schuster Children's Publishing Division

1230 Avenue of the Americas, New York, New York 10020

Copyright © 2013 by Simon & Schuster, Inc.

All rights reserved, including the right of reproduction
in whole or in part in any form.

SIMON SPOTLIGHT and colophon are registered
trademarks of Simon & Schuster, Inc.

Text by Tracey West

Chapter header illustrations by Chuyi Wu

Designed by Laura Roode

For information about special discounts for bulk purchases, please contact
Simon & Schuster Special Sales
at 1-866-506-1949 or business@simonandschuster.com.

Manufactured in the United States of America 1213 OFF

First Edition 2 4 6 8 10 9 7 5 3

ISBN 978-1-4424-7435-2 (pbk)

ISBN 978-1-4424-7480-2 (hc)

ISBN 978-1-4424-7436-9 (eBook)

Library of Congress Catalog Card Number 2013935693

CUPCAKE DIARIES

Mia
a
matter
of
taste

by coco simon

Simon Spotlight

New York   London   Toronto   Sydney   New Delhi

CHAPTER 1

The Worst News Ever

"Okay, Mia, open wide."

"Open wide" might be two of the scariest words in the English language, don't you think? Because when you hear them, it usually means a dentist is about to look into your mouth.

Not that I have anything against dentists. My dentist is Dr. Brown, though I normally call her Mrs. Brown since she is my friend Katie's mom. She's supernice, and I'm sure most dentists are perfectly nice people. I just don't like the stuff they have to do.

Anyway, the person asking me to open wide wasn't even Mrs. Brown. It was her assistant Joanne, who is also really nice. She's tall, and she wears her blond hair up in a ponytail all the time, and under her blue scrubs I can always tell that her clothes are very fashionable.

Joanne must have noticed the nervous look on my face.

"It's cool, Mia. I'm just taking some X-rays. This doesn't hurt at all. You know that, right?" she asked.

I nodded. "Okay."

I opened wide, and Joanne stuck this white square thing into my mouth and told me to bite down. Then she straightened the heavy gray apron covering me and left the room. I heard a quick buzz, and then Joanne came back in and took out the square thing.

"You know, this really isn't that flattering," I joked, looking down at the apron.

She laughed. "Just a few more shots and you can take it off, and then you'll be ready for the runway again, okay?"

Joanne was right—the X-rays didn't hurt at all, but I was glad when they were over.

"Dr. Brown will be by in a minute to go over them with you," Joanne told me. "I'll send in your mom, okay?"

"Thanks," I said, and inside I felt a little bit relieved. Up until a couple of years ago, I lived in Manhattan. Mom and Dad worked during the day, and my babysitter always took me to the dentist. Now we live in the suburbs, and Mom mostly works from home and has her own company, so she has more time to do stuff like this. It's nice having her around, especially at the dentist's.

"How'd it go?" Mom asked as she came into the room.

"My teeth are superclean," I said, flashing her a smile. "And Joanne said it doesn't look like I have any cavities. So I'm thinking I deserve some kind of reward for being so awesome."

Mom raised an eyebrow. "You want a reward for not getting any cavities?"

"I was thinking a trip to the mall would be good," I said.

"Well, you don't have to twist my arm for that," Mom replied. I guess it's a good thing we both love shopping!

Then Mrs. Brown came in. She has the same friendly brown eyes as my friend Katie, but Mrs. Brown's light brown hair is cut short, with long bangs that are stylishly angled across her face.

"It looks like you're cavity free, Mia, but let me take a look in person, okay?"

I nodded and opened my mouth again until she was done.

"Very good," she said with a nod. Then she looked at me, and then at my mom. "But we should talk about your X-rays."

She pressed some keys on the computer on the table next to me, and the pictures of my mouth popped up. It was really weird to see how long the roots were underneath my gums, and I turned my head away. My teeth looked too creepy!

"Mia's got some crooked teeth on her bottom jaw, and her top jaw as well," Mrs. Brown said, pointing to the screen with the end of her pen. "Her bite is misaligned, which can cause problems down the road. I'm recommending you see an orthodontist. I'm not sure, but Mia may need braces."

A cold chill went right through me.

"Braces? Seriously?" I asked. It sounded more like I was squeaking, because I was so upset.

"Well, as I said, I'm not one hundred percent sure," Mrs. Brown said. "But it's very likely."

I looked up at my mom. I could already feel my eyes starting to well up with tears. I started shaking my head. "No way! I can*not* get braces. I will die!"

"Mia, it's okay," Mom assured, putting her hand on my shoulder.

Mrs. Brown gave me a sympathetic look. "I

4

understand. Nobody wants to hear news like this. But by correcting your teeth now, we can help make sure your mouth stays healthy for a long, long time. I have some brochures I'll give you, so you can find out what it's all about."

Then she turned to my mom. "I know a great orthodontist over in River Glen. I'll get you her card." She smiled at me. "She's the same doctor Katie used when she had her braces."

Mrs. Brown left, and I looked at Mom. "Please tell me this isn't happening!"

"There's no need to panic yet, Mia," Mom said. "Let's wait and see what the orthodontist says before we start worrying, okay? And anyway, braces aren't so bad. Katie had them! And your cousin Marcela had them, remember?"

Marcela is a junior in high school now, but she had braces when she was my age. I definitely remembered them. How could I forget a mouth full of metal and wires? I shuddered.

"She was always complaining that they hurt," I pointed out. "And when we all went to that farm she couldn't eat a candy apple, and she cried."

"That's just what you remember. I know that most of the time, she was fine," Mom said, and then she quickly changed the subject. "Hey, we should

5

get out of here and get to the mall!"

Mom's strategy worked—at first. I never get tired of going to the mall. Since my dentist appointment was right after school, I was kind of hungry, so Mom got me a vanilla mango smoothie at Smoothie Paradise. I sipped the delicious tropical goodness through a straw as we slowly walked around, window-shopping.

"Well, if I get braces, at least I can still have smoothies," I remarked, and Mom smiled.

"That sounds more like my Mia. Stay positive!"

But I ruined my own mood by bringing up the braces, and it didn't even help when we went inside Icon, my favorite shop in the whole mall. They had all the new summer styles on the racks, in tons of bright, almost fluorescent colors.

I held up a neon-yellow sleeveless dress. "Wow, you could wear this in the dark and people could see you for miles," I said. I actually look good in yellow, so I brought the dress to the mirror and held it up to my face.

I posed and smiled, and then suddenly I got a vision of myself in the bright yellow dress with a mouth full of blinding silver metal.

"I can't wear this if I get braces!" I wailed. "It's too much! Aliens in space will be able to see me."

"Oh, Mia, that's not true," Mom said, trying to reassure me, but it was no use.

"If I get stupid braces, I won't be able to wear any of the new summer styles!" I complained. "I might as well go live under a rock somewhere!"

Mom sighed. "Come on, let's go to the candle shop. I think you need some calming scents."

I could feel tears stinging my eyes as I followed Mom out of Icon. And the scent of misty mountain sandalwood candles (my favorite) did not help one bit. I was convinced braces were going to ruin my life!

CHAPTER 2

My Friends Are the Best!

The next morning I had a soccer game, but I couldn't concentrate at all. The coach had me playing fullback, and twice I let one of the players from the other team breeze right past me to the goal. They scored both times! It's a good thing my friend Emma is on my team, because she's a really good and fast player, and she scored two goals to make up for it. In the end, we won by one point.

After the game, Emma and I found her dad over on the sidelines. He has dark blond hair and blue eyes, just like Emma and all the rest of the Taylors. They're one of those families where it's easy to tell that they're all related.

"What time is your cupcake meeting?" Mr. Taylor asked us as we piled into the minivan.

"Katie and Alexis are coming over at eleven thirty," Emma replied, nodding to the clock on the dashboard, which read 10:56. "We've got plenty of time."

I guess I was so upset about hearing that I might need braces that I forgot to tell you about the Cupcake Club. Sorry! My friends Katie, Alexis, Emma, and I formed the club when we started middle school. At first we did it just so we could hang out and bake cupcakes, but it's turned into a real business. So we have regular meetings, and we're always busy baking cupcakes and making displays for the parties we do.

"Good. You girls will have time to test out the granola bars I made this morning," Emma's dad said. "With the four Taylors all in sports, I'm spending all my money on protein bars."

"Hey, that's Matt and Sam's fault," Emma said, bringing up her two older brothers. "They're both bottomless pits."

Mr. Taylor winked into the rearview mirror. "You do pretty good yourself, Emma. But that's okay. You're all growing kids."

Emma looked at me and rolled her eyes. Parents always say the goofiest things!

A few minutes later we were sitting at Emma's

kitchen table, munching on Mr. Taylor's homemade granola bars. They were nutty, with some bits of dark chocolate in them, and very crunchy.

"So, what do you think?" Emma's dad asked.

"They're good," I said.

Emma nodded. "Maybe a little bit dry, though."

Mr. Taylor looked thoughtful. "Maybe I should add more yogurt."

"You should ask Katie," I suggested. "She's really good at fixing recipes."

"Hey, thanks!"

Katie came into the kitchen with a big smile on her face, followed by Alexis. Katie was wearing a white T-shirt with a picture of a unicorn on it, and purple shorts. Alexis had her curly red hair pulled back with a blue headband that matched the cute top she was wearing, along with some skinny jeans. I was feeling pretty unfashionable in my soccer uniform.

Mr. Taylor handed a granola bar to each of them. "Testing out a new recipe. I'm accepting criticism."

"We will give you a full report later, Dad," Emma said. "Right now, we've got important cupcake business to conduct."

"Okay, I can take a hint!" Mr. Taylor said as he backed out of the room.

Katie and Alexis slid into seats at the kitchen table with us.

"So how was the game?" Alexis asked.

"We won!" Emma reported happily.

I made a face. "No thanks to me," I said. "I was off my game this morning."

"You were fine," Emma said, trying to make me feel better.

I shook my head. "No, I was distracted," I said, and then I decided to break my big news. "I found out yesterday that I might need to get braces!"

"No way!" Katie exclaimed, surprised. "My mom didn't say anything to me about it."

"Well, she really can't," Alexis pointed out. "Doctor-patient confidentiality."

"I have to go see the orthodontist," I continued. "Then I'll know for sure."

"Well, maybe Katie's mom is wrong," Emma said. "My dentist said I might need braces, but the orthodontist said I didn't."

I turned to Katie. "Gee, I hope your mom is a terrible dentist!"

Emma turned bright red, but thankfully, Katie just laughed.

"It's okay. I hope she's wrong too," Katie said. "I mean, who wants to get braces?"

Emma's oldest brother, Sam, walked into the room. Katie and I both have a little crush on him, even though he's in high school, so we know crushing on him is just ridiculous. But it's hard *not* to like him. It's not just that he has awesome wavy blond hair or that he's a star on the basketball team, but he's supernice.

Sam opened the refrigerator and then took out a carton of milk. "Who needs braces?" he asked.

I raised my hand. "Me. Probably. Hopefully not."

"I had them," Sam said. "They're not that bad."

I couldn't imagine someone as cute as Sam having braces.

"You used to complain all the time about how much they hurt," Emma reminded him.

"That was just to get extra ice cream from Mom," Sam said. "Seriously, Mia, they hurt for a while when you first get them adjusted, but most of the time you can hardly feel them."

"Thanks," I said. "That makes me feel better." And honestly, it did.

Sam chugged right from the milk carton and then threw the empty carton into the garbage can. "Man, Dad's protein bars are superdry!"

I waited until Sam left to confess my major fear to my friends.

12

"It's not just the hurting stuff that bothers me," I said. "Can you imagine me with a mouth full of metal? That is fashion death."

"You know," Alexis said, "you can get those clear braces. They don't show as much."

Katie agreed. "Yeah, I've heard Mom talk about how popular they're getting."

"Oh my gosh, I totally forgot about those!" I said. "I could maybe deal with braces if they were clear."

It was like I suddenly saw a rainbow in a stormy sky. I went from hopeless to hopeful in less than ten seconds. Aren't my friends great? They always know exactly how to make me feel better.

"So, anyway," Alexis said, "we need to get ready for that party tomorrow."

"We're doing three dozen, right?" Katie asked, and Alexis nodded.

"I dropped off the frosting colors here last night," I offered.

Emma stood up. "Let me just clear off Dad's granola bar mess, so we can start baking."

The cupcakes we were baking were our most basic combination—vanilla cupcakes with vanilla icing—but they were going to look really special when we decorated them. As we started the batter, we talked about the party that was coming up.

"I can't believe we're running another kids' party," Katie said, making a face. She's an only child—like I was before I got my stepbrother—so she freaks out around little kids sometimes. But Katie is sweet and fun, so she's actually really good with kids. They love her! She's just got to get used to them, I think.

"It's good for business," Alexis pointed out. "For any business to grow, it needs to branch out."

"Besides, this is going to be a fun party," Emma added. "It's so cool the twins wanted a music-dance theme."

"How do they know what they want? They're only four," Katie said. "When I was four, I wanted to be a dinosaur."

"Come on, Katie, all little kids like music," I said.

One of the moms from our school, Mrs. Watson, had approached us at a PTA dinner about throwing a party for her twins, who were turning five. Alexis followed up with a phone call, and when she found out that the twins loved music, she came up with the dance party idea. We'd have a dance floor and do fun dance contests and teach them some silly dances we looked up online, like the Pony. (That's basically when you move your feet up and down

14

in one place, like you're galloping, and hold your hands in front of you, like you're pretending to ride a horse.)

And, of course, there would be cupcakes. Even though they were plain vanilla cakes, we were doing the icing in different colors and arranging them to look like one of those cool light-up dance floors. Then I was going to pipe music notes on them with black frosting.

"Mia, did you make that playlist for the party?" Alexis asked.

"Yep. I got a list of the twins' favorite songs from Mrs. Watson, plus, I downloaded some of those songs to go with the special dances."

Alexis nodded. "Good. I brought a checklist we can go over when we're done."

A couple of hours later we had three dozen perfect cupcakes safely stored in the special cupcake carriers we use, and Alexis had checked off every single box on her checklist.

"I can't believe how organized we are for this party," she said, looking really happy. "This is going to be our most perfect event yet."

Emma made a face. "Don't jinx it!"

"Anyway, we still need to practice," Katie added.

"Practice what?" Alexis asked.

"Our dancing!" Katie replied. "Come on, let's do the Twist!"

She started twisting her hips from side to side. We all joined in, dancing around Emma's kitchen, until her other older brother, Matt, walked in.

"Girls!" he said, rolling his eyes, and we started laughing so hard, we couldn't dance anymore. And for the first time in twenty-four hours, I wasn't even thinking about braces. That's how awesome my friends are!

CHAPTER 3

Heavy Metal Mayhem

The four of us got to Mrs. Watson's house to set up for the party at ten the next morning. Luckily, it was a beautiful spring day with no chance of rain.

"Oh, the cupcakes are perfect!" said Mrs. Watson, a friendly looking woman with a round face and curly blond hair. "All my friends are going to want to hire you for their parties!"

"Thank you," Alexis said, and then she turned to us and gave us an *I told you so* look.

I pointed to a blue canopy that had been erected over the lawn in the backyard.

"Is that where we can set up the dance area?" I asked.

Mrs. Watson nodded. "I thought that would be best. And please just put all the cupcakes on the table on the deck with the rest of the food."

"Perfect!" Alexis said, and I knew she just loved hearing the sound of that word. "We'll take care of everything."

Emma and Katie brought the cupcakes up to the deck, leaving them covered until the party started. Then we all got to work decorating the dance area. We tied balloons to the poles holding up the canopy, and then we took out cardboard music notes I had cut out and covered with glitter. We hung those with strings from the support poles underneath the canopy. We had to stand on chairs to do it, but it was worth the effort.

"Ooh, this looks so amazing!" Emma said, stepping back to admire it all.

"It's perfect!" Alexis said, emphasizing the word again.

Emma frowned. "We can't say it's perfect until it's over."

Alexis shook her head. "You're just being superstitious. We can be confident because we are organized. That's the beauty of organization."

"I just need to set up the music," I said, and Katie helped me find an outlet so I could plug in my iPod speakers.

When it was almost time for the party to start,

Mrs. Watson brought the twins over to meet us.

"Claire and John, meet Alexis, Emma, Katie, and Mia," their mom said, introducing us. To go with the music theme, the twins wore T-shirts—John's was blue and Claire's was green—with music notes on them. They both had the same green eyes and light brown hair. There's just something super adorable about twins. Their cute factor sky-rocketed when they started to talk.

"We're going to have a party!" John informed us, excited.

"Yeah, and we're going to dance!" Claire said, and then she began bopping up and down. Her brother started dancing with her.

"Oh my gosh, you guys are soooo cute!" Emma cooed.

Katie leaned over and whispered to me. "I have to admit it, they are pretty adorable."

I grinned. "Maybe this party will be perfect after all."

The place quickly started filling with kids—twenty in total. At first I was worried it might be too much for us, but Alexis was right. We had the party organized really well, and things went smoothly. First, Emma did this craft where the kids used beans and recycled containers to make fun shakers. Then we helped Mrs. Watson feed the kids round sandwiches that looked like CDs. Finally, it was time for the big dance party.

Alexis and I stayed on the deck to clean up the food while Katie and Emma kicked things off.

"Everyone under the tent!" Katie yelled. "It's time for the dance party!"

The kids ran like crazy to the canopy and started to jump up and down. Emma called up, "Mia, which playlist do I choose?"

"It's the one called 'party playlist,'" I called back down to her.

"Thanks!" Emma turned on the speakers, selected the playlist, and hit play.

Then a sound like a pack of wild dogs barking in a thunderstorm filled the backyard.

"We are the army of the night! We will always stand and fight!"

Emma's blue eyes got wide, and she sort of froze. Alexis started screaming, "Turn it off! Turn it off!" After about three of the longest seconds ever, Emma snapped out of it and shut off the iPod.

The kids were confused, and Mrs. Watson ran up to Alexis.

"What on Earth was that terrible racket?" she asked.

And then the horrible truth hit me: I had taken the wrong iPod off the charging station in the kitchen this morning. This had to be my stepbrother's, Dan's. Our iPods look the same, but the contents are different; he constantly listens to heavy metal music.

"Oh no!" I cried. "I'm so sorry. It's the wrong iPod."

"Well, where is the right one?" Alexis asked.

I thought quickly. "It might still be home. Let me call my mom."

I dialed her number and started talking a mile a minute when she picked up.

"Mom it's an emergency I took Dan's iPod by mistake and left mine at home and if I don't have my iPod the whole party is going to be ruined!"

Luckily, Mom understands me when I talk that fast. "I'll be right there, Mia. Text me the address."

I obeyed and put my phone away, relieved. "Mom will be here with my iPod soon," I told Alexis.

"Okay. But what will we do until then?" she asked, nodding to the kids below. They were starting to get wild, running all over the yard.

Think fast, Mia, I told myself. *This is your fault. You've got to fix it.*

And then I figured it out. "We don't need an iPod to make music. Come on."

I grabbed Alexis by the hand, and we ran down the stairs into the yard. Then I started to sing the first song I could think of.

"The wheels on the bus go round and round, round and round . . ."

Katie, Alexis, and Emma got the idea and began to sing along with me. We went around the yard, grabbing kids by the hand and leading them back under the canopy. Then we started doing the hand motions to the song, and the kids joined in.

That lasted about a minute. "What next?" Alexis hissed.

Luckily, Emma started wiggling her fingers in twinkly motions and singing "Twinkle, Twinkle Little Star." We sang that one a good five times before the kids got tired of it.

Next, Alexis remembered a song from when she was in preschool about popcorn. "Pop! Pop! Pop! Put it in the pot!" For that one we got everyone to dance up and down like they were pieces of popping popcorn, and the kids loved it.

"I can't think of any songs!" Katie wailed when the kids were tired of popping. Then her face lit up. "Hey, who wants to do the Pony?"

The kids all raised their hands, and Katie started to dance. She started singing a crazy tune and making up her own words.

"Do the Pony, yeah, yeah, yeah. It's really fun! Yeah, yeah, yeah!"

I thought we were going to have to start with "Wheels on the Bus" all over again when I saw Mom walking into the driveway. I ran up to her.

"You are the best!" I said, giving her a hug.

She handed me the iPod. "Put this in, and then bring me Dan's. He's been a little cranky this morning. He can't go ten minutes without his heavy metal."

I quickly replaced Dan's iPod with mine and started the correct party playlist. A Wiggles song started blasting through the speakers, and the kids all cheered. The party was saved! I gave Mom a big hug and thanked her. She watched for a while, smiling at us, then winked and headed out.

The rest of the party went really smoothly. The kids loved the dance party we planned, and then we helped Mrs. Watson serve the birthday cupcakes. When we were cleaning up, she approached us with an envelope. I suddenly felt nervous.

"Uh-oh," I whispered to Katie. "I wonder if she's going to be upset about the music mix-up."

"She looks happy," Katie whispered back.

And she was. "Thank you so much for all your hard work," she said, handing Alexis the envelope. "Here's your payment. Claire and John and all their friends had such a good time."

Still, I felt bad. "Sorry about blasting that loud music."

Mrs. Watson smiled. "No problem. Plus, no party is ever perfect. But everyone here had a perfectly good time. I was impressed with how you handled the situation. You might think about adding musical entertainment to your list of party skills. "

"I'd rather stick to cupcakes," Katie piped up.

"We aim to please," Alexis said quickly, handing her a small stack of our business cards. "Please recommend us to your friends."

"I certainly will," Mrs. Watson replied. "Or I might just hire you for the cupcakes. It looks like we won't have any extras!" She turned around, and we saw Mr. Watson with a cupcake in each hand.

"That happens a lot!" said Alexis.

Then Alexis's mom came by to pick us all up. As we were loading our stuff into the car, Katie said, "That was really fun."

"It was," I agreed. I looked at Alexis. "I'm sorry it wasn't perfect."

"That's okay," Alexis said. "It turned out all right in the end."

"That's right," Emma agreed. "Things don't have to be perfect to be great."

I didn't think much about what Emma said at the time. But a few weeks later, those words would become really important to me.

CHAPTER 4

I Can See Just Fine! Sort Of . . .

The party on Sunday put me in such a good mood, I almost forgot that I might need braces—almost. But Mom said my orthodontist appointment wasn't, like, for a week, so I decided to put it out of my mind.

The next day was Monday, a school day, and it was one of those beautiful, warm spring days that makes you wish you were anywhere except inside school. On the bus ride that morning, Katie and I took turns saying where we'd rather be.

"Window-shopping in SoHo in Manhattan," I said.

"Walking on the beach in bare feet," said Katie.

"Eating a croissant at a café in Paris."

"Eating a tamale from a cart in Mexico City."

"Scuba diving in a coral reef."

"Running in a beautiful shady park."

Then the bus pulled to a stop in front of the school.

"I guess we'll have to settle for math class with Mr. K.," Katie said, and we both laughed.

Katie and I have math together first period, right after homeroom. On the first day of school Mr. K. (his name is Mr. Kazinski, but most of the kids call him Mr. K.) let us sit wherever we wanted, so Katie and I found two seats together in the third row. When we got there today, Mr. K. was writing a bunch of equations on the board.

I had to squint to make them out. "Wow, Mr. K. has terrible handwriting," I whispered to Katie. "I can't read any of those numbers."

Katie got a funny look on her face. "They look just fine to me," she said. "Are you having trouble seeing things again?"

"What do you mean?" I asked.

"I mean, a couple of weeks ago when we went to the movies, you were squinting too," Katie said. "Remember? And then you made us sit all the way up front."

I hadn't really thought about it. "Yeah, I guess. But I think there was something wrong with the projector. Things looked kind of blurry to me."

Katie didn't say anything, and then the bell rang, and class started.

"Morning, everybody," Mr. K. said. He's a pretty easygoing teacher, a tall guy with sandy-blond hair and wire-rimmed glasses. "Today we're going to review turning fractions into decimals." He touched a pointer to a fraction he had written on the board. "Mia, can you please tell me the equation for turning this number into a fraction?"

I squinted again. "I'm sorry, I can't read your writing. Is that eight over thirty-nine?"

Mr. K. gave me a funny look and then glanced back at the board. "Hmm. I always try to print clearly. Maybe you just need a better view. Randall, switch desks with Mia, please."

I gave Katie a desperate look, but there was nothing I could do. I gathered my stuff together and moved to Randall Mitchell's seat in the very center of the front row. Then I sat down.

"Better?" Mr. K. asked.

I looked at the board again. "Oh! It's three over twenty. So that would be three divided by twenty, which is . . . point fifteen."

"Right," said Mr. K. "So did you see how Mia did that?" And then he began to write it out.

I was kind of proud of myself for getting the answer right like that. But I wasn't happy with my new seat. I thought about raising my hand and asking Mr. K. if I could move back to the third row, but I didn't want to draw any more attention to myself, you know?

The next morning, Randall was sitting in his usual seat in the front row, so I just sat down in my seat next to Katie, and Mr. K. didn't say anything about it. And it didn't matter, anyway, because we worked in our math workbooks for the whole class.

Tuesday night we had a Cupcake Club meeting at Katie's house. Katie's mom made us beans and rice and guacamole for dinner, because Katie became crazy for Mexican food after she took a summer cooking class. I put extra hot sauce on my food because I like things spicy.

I looked at Alexis and held up the bottle. "Want some?" A few weeks ago, Alexis took a challenge to try some spicy food that my stepdad cooked. She was brave and tried it, but she didn't like it much.

She stuck her tongue out at me. "Very funny! Besides, Mrs. Brown's food is delicious just the way it is."

"Why, thank you, Alexis," Katie's mom said, looking up from her plate. Then she turned to me.

"Mia, I hear that you're going to see Dr. Payne next Wednesday."

I dropped my fork. "Dr. *Pain*? Are you kidding me? That's my orthodontist's name?"

Mrs. Brown sighed. "It's Payne, P-A-Y-N-E. Poor Melanie. It's definitely an unfortunate name for an orthodontist."

"I would change it if I were her," Alexis said. "That's got to be bad for business."

"Her work speaks for itself," Katie's mom said. "Don't worry, Mia. You will be in very good hands with Dr. Payne, no matter what happens."

I couldn't finish my dinner. I kept imagining a scary-looking woman with black eyes and a thin, sharp face, leaning over me with jagged silver tools and saying those two horrible words: "Open wide!"

When we finished dinner and helped clean up, Mrs. Brown left us in the kitchen for our meeting. Alexis took out her laptop and started the meeting like she usually does.

"Our next big Cupcake job is the carnival," she announced. "Principal LaCosta said we can set up a Cupcake Club booth and sell our cupcakes. Since it's a big event, we've got to leave everyone with a good impression."

"Maybe a summer theme?" Emma suggested.

I kind of liked that. "We could decorate the cupcakes to look like beach balls. That would be cute."

"Cute is nice, but we need fantastic!" Alexis reminded us. "Something memorable. Different. Something that hasn't been done before."

We all sat around for a while, thinking. The kitchen got eerily quiet.

"I can't think of anything," Katie finally said. "My mind is empty."

"Mine too," Emma agreed.

We were all quiet again. Then Katie got up and turned on the radio in the kitchen.

"What are you doing?" Alexis asked.

"Getting some inspiration," Katie said. She began to dance around the kitchen. She grabbed my hand, and then Alexis's and Emma's, and got us off our chairs. Soon we were all dancing around and giggling.

"I'm not getting any inspiration," Emma said. "But I don't care!"

"Me either!" Katie said, laughing.

So we didn't get anything else done at our cupcake meeting. And you know what? That was just fine. Sometimes we just needed to take a break and have some fun.

31

CHAPTER 5

More Bad News

I spent the weekend at my dad's in Manhattan. (My parents are divorced, so I stay with him every other weekend.) Lately the weekends are a little stressful because Dad's got a new girlfriend. I have to admit that Lynne is pretty nice, but she's got a son, Ethan, who's five, and he's okay and everything, but he's very whiny and cranky and cries all the time. So my weekends with Dad just aren't the same.

But that weekend I was happy to get away because my appointment with Dr. Payne was coming up, and I couldn't stop thinking about it. I didn't even mind when we all went to the movies and Ethan somehow managed to get a half-chewed gummy worm stuck in my hair. Totally gross, I know, but it definitely got my mind off getting braces!

But the weekend was over quickly, and before I knew it, it was Wednesday and I was sitting in Dr. Payne's waiting room with Mom and Eddie, my stepdad.

I guess I got lucky when I got Eddie for a stepdad. He's nothing like my real dad, and he'll never replace him. But he's really, really nice to my mom and me, and we love him and he loves us. And he's always trying to crack us up with jokes.

I have to admit, though, that sitting in the doctor's office, I was getting kind of annoyed with Eddie's humor.

"Getting braces won't be so bad," Eddie was saying. "I knew a kid once who could pick up radio signals on his."

"You did not!" Mom said.

"Just great. So you're saying I'll be a total freak," I said, and my eyes started to get hot with tears.

"Oh, Mia, honey, I didn't mean that," Eddie said, and I could tell he felt bad. Mom gave him a look and a poke.

Then a young guy in scrubs came into the waiting room. "Mia?" he called out, and Mom nodded. "Dr. Payne will see you now."

"I'll stay out here," Eddie said, patting his stomach. "I've been eating too many of Mia's cupcakes. I probably won't fit."

So Mom and I followed the guy into the exam room. I sat in the big metal chair. There were pictures of waterfalls and forests and things on the wall, and I guess they were there to help make patients feel peaceful or something. But there was also a tray full of sharp metal tools, and that sort of canceled out the peaceful pictures.

"I'm Louis," the assistant said. "I'll set you up, and then Dr. Payne will be right in."

He put one of those paper bibs around my neck and tilted my chair back. A few seconds later a woman in a white doctor's coat entered the room. She didn't look evil, like the Dr. Payne in my imagination. She had curly hair that she wore pulled back, green eyes, and freckles across her nose. She kind of looked a little bit like Alexis, all grown up, and I almost laughed. I could kind of see Alexis becoming an orthodontist.

"I'm Dr. Payne," she said, smiling. "It's nice to meet you, Mia."

"Thanks," I replied. I know I should have said "Nice to meet you, too," but I wasn't so sure about that yet.

"So, I've looked at your X-rays," she said. "Now I'd like to take a look in person, if that's okay."

"You mean I have a choice?" I asked.

Dr. Payne smiled. "Always. But I think you know you're here for a good reason, Mia. Braces can help you keep your teeth healthy for a long, long time."

She had this really calm voice, almost like she was hypnotizing me.

"Okay," I said, and then I opened my mouth.

Dr. Payne looked around, and even took two more X-rays. Then she came back in. I crossed my fingers on both hands.

"Mia, Dr. Brown was right. I would definitely recommend braces for you."

Deep down, I knew that's what she was going to say. But I was still shocked. I started to cry right away.

"Really?" I asked.

"Yes," said Dr. Payne. "You'll probably need to wear them for a year, maybe more."

"A *year*?" I knew I was loud, but I didn't care. I was totally freaking out. Mom put her hand on my arm.

"Mia, it's going to be okay," she said. "Let's let Dr. Payne explain things to us."

Dr. Payne started going on and on about where

the braces would go and something about a retainer, but I wasn't really listening. She took out a model of teeth with silver braces on them. Then I remembered something.

"Can't I get the clear ones at least?" I blurted out.

"Well, there are pros and cons," Dr. Payne said. "The pro is that they're not as noticeable. The cons are that they can take longer to work than the metal braces, and they can be more expensive, too. They don't work for everyone, but I think you'd be a good candidate."

"Please, Mom? Please?" I begged.

Mom looked flustered. "I need to talk this over with your father." She looked at Dr. Payne. "Do you need a decision right away?"

"There's no real rush," the doctor replied. "I'll give you the literature for both, and you can call me anytime if you have questions."

When I walked back into the waiting room, Eddie knew just by looking at me what had happened.

"Bad news, huh?" he asked, and all I could do was nod.

Mom took care of the paperwork, and then we all piled into Eddie's car. Nobody said anything for a few minutes, and then Mom said, "Hon, where are we going?"

Eddie just smiled, and a minute later we pulled into the parking lot of King Cone, the ice-cream place in our town. There's no inside; just a window where you get your ice cream and then picnic benches where you can sit and eat outside. It's open every year from St. Patrick's Day until Halloween. My favorite part is the giant plastic ice-cream cone with a crown and a smiling face that's out front.

"It's a perfect day for ice cream," Eddie said, and I knew he meant more than it was just nice out. He was trying to cheer me up. Eddie's really good with stuff like that.

I was acting like I was still miserable, but deep down I was happy about getting ice cream.

"Mia, what do you want?" Eddie asked.

"Vanilla ice cream with hot fudge," I mumbled.

Eddie grinned at the woman at the counter. "One small vanilla cone for my lovely lady here; one small hot fudge sundae for this other lovely lady; and for me, a cup of chocolate ice cream with rainbow sprinkles, chocolate syrup, and gummy bears."

I smiled for the first time since I got the news about my braces.

"Seriously?" I asked him.

"It's an excellent combination," Eddie assured me. "I'll let you try some."

"No, thanks," I said, shaking my head.

Soon we were all seated around a red plastic picnic table, eating our ice cream. The sky was bright blue with perfect cotton-ball clouds floating around in it. My hot fudge sundae was delicious, and the fudge was nice and warm while the ice cream was supercold. Yum!

"Oh man, this is delicious!" Eddie said, smiling. Then Mom and I started cracking up. He had gummy bears stuck all over his teeth!

"What's so funny?" Eddie asked, and that made us laugh even harder.

Finally, Mom was able to speak. "Sweetie, you've got gummy bears stuck in your teeth."

Eddie ran his tongue across his teeth. "Oh man. See? I don't even have braces and I've got stuff stuck in my teeth!"

"They look like rainbow braces," I said, giggling. "I bet Katie would like those."

Eddie took another bite, shaking his head. "I'm going to have to think of another combination."

So Eddie being funny wasn't annoying anymore. I felt a little bit better—just a teeny, tiny, little bit.

Eddie

Chris

CHAPTER 6

Sooooo Embarrassing!

So it's official. I have to get braces," I announced at lunch the next day.

"Oh, I'm so sorry, Mia," Emma said sympathetically.

"Mom's going to talk to Dad about getting me the clear ones," I said. "So keep your fingers crossed for me."

"But don't you have to keep those on longer?" Katie asked. "I'd rather just get the metal and get it over with."

"It all depends," I replied. "But, anyway, I'd rather look normal but be uncomfortable for years than look like a metal mouth for one day."

"The metal ones really aren't that bad," Alexis said. "I remember when Emma's brother had his.

After a while, I didn't even notice them on Sam."

Emma nodded. "True. And it didn't stop girls from walking by our house to look at him, either, like they always do. Gross."

"Well, I'd be happier with the clear," I said, starting to feel slightly annoyed.

"Of course!" Katie said quickly. She held up both hands. "See? I'm crossing *all* my fingers."

Then George Martinez walked up to our table. He's in our grade, and he and Katie have been friends for a long time. His dark hair is short and kind of curly, and he has really nice brown eyes.

"Katie, are you having finger issues?" he asked.

Katie laughed and quickly lowered her hands. "No. Just wishing for something, that's all."

"So, do you guys want to go to the park after school?" he asked. I know he said "you guys," but we all knew he mostly wanted Katie to be there. They both like each other, and sometimes I wonder if they're boyfriend and girlfriend, but Katie always says no, they're just friends.

Katie looked around the table. "Are you guys busy?"

"I've got a Future Business Leaders of America meeting," Alexis said.

"And I've got some dog walking to do," Emma

answered. "But I guess I could walk them in the park and come by and hang out with you guys for a while."

"I can go," I told Katie.

She nodded to George. "See you there."

George left, and Alexis leaned in.

"Wow, Katie. He practically asked you out on a date!" she said.

Katie blushed. "Hanging out at the park isn't a date. Besides, he asked all of us."

"That reminds me," I said. "This carnival coming up. Do you have to, like, go with 'somebody,' or can you just go with friends?"

"I think you can just go with friends," Emma replied. "That's what Matt did last year."

I felt relieved. The only boy in school I'm interested in is Chris Howard. He's tall, handsome, and kind of quiet, and nice. We went to the pep rally parade together. You had to wear costumes, so I dressed up like a witch, and he dressed up like a warlock. We even held hands.

That was a while ago. After the pep rally, Chris asked me to go to the movies and I said no. Not because I don't like him, but because it just felt too much like a real date, you know? And, honestly, I don't know if I'm ready for that yet. Going to school together is nice enough for now. But ever since I turned him down, Chris doesn't talk to me as much. I think maybe I hurt his feelings, and I feel kind of bad about that, because that's not what I meant to do.

"We still need a cupcake idea for the carnival," Alexis reminded us.

Katie frowned. "I am having a hard time thinking of something! But I'll keep trying."

"And we've got one job this weekend," Alexis added. "Two dozen lemon cupcakes for a baby shower. We're baking at my house on Friday night. Emma and Mia have a soccer game Saturday morning so, Katie, can you deliver with me?"

Katie nodded. "Sure. Only, my mom's working, so can yours drive?"

Alexis quickly typed into her smartphone. "I'll make a note, but I think she can. Or my dad will."

We finished up our cupcake business before it was time to go to our next classes. When the final bell of the day rang, I met Katie at her locker, and we headed outside to the park.

"Who else do you think is going to be there?" I asked, and Katie shrugged.

"I'm not sure. George has a lot of friends," she replied, and it was true. George is one of those kids who isn't just friends with people in one group. He gets along with everybody.

When we got to the park, we saw George over by the swings with Ken Watanabe, his best friend, and another boy named Chau Tran, who Katie says is funny and nice. Our friends Sophie and Lucy were on the steps by the slide. I was secretly hoping Chris would be there, but I didn't see him.

"Yo!" George called out, waving when he saw us, and we walked over. I noticed that Ken was lying on his back on the bottom of the slide, and he looked kind of pale.

"Is he okay?" I asked.

"He was trying to break the land speed record on the merry-go-round," Chau reported. "It didn't go well."

Katie shuddered. "I can't go on that thing. It makes me too dizzy! The swings are much better."

She sat down in one, and George got behind her and gave her a push.

"Awww, how sweet!" Sophie teased, and Katie blushed a little.

I got on the swing next to Katie and started to swing too. We all started talking about school, and then George did this impression of Ms. Chen, our gym teacher, that had us cracking up.

I was still swinging when I noticed two boys playing basketball in the court on the opposite side of the park. I put my hand over my eyes and squinted. One of them was Chris Howard!

I guess I was feeling kind of giddy from being on the swings and laughing and everything, so I started waving my arms and yelling, "Yo, Chris! Over here! Hey!"

"Mia, what are you doing?" Katie asked.

Chris tossed the ball to his friend and started walking over to the swings.

"That's not Chris," Katie said. "That's Eddie Rossi."

I squinted and realized she was right. Eddie is tall, like Chris, and he's nice and everything, but he mostly hangs out with the girls in the Best Friends Club.

"Oh no!" I wailed. "What do I do?"

"I have no idea," Katie replied.

Eddie walked up to me with a big grin on his face. "Hi, Mia. What's up?"

"Um, hi, I mean, nothing," I said, and I felt my face getting red. Did Eddie think I liked him? I should have told him I thought he was Chris, but I was too embarrassed. Luckily, Ken saved me. He sat up and walked over to Eddie.

"Dude, push me on that thing," he said, nodding toward the merry-go-round. "I think I can go faster."

Chau shook his head. "Some people never learn," he said, but he and George ran to watch.

I was off the hook. Then Emma came up to us, walking a big, yellow lab on a leash.

"Hey," she said. "What's happening?"

"Only the most embarrassing moment of my life!" I replied dramatically.

"It wasn't that bad," Katie said. "She just thought Eddie Rossi was Chris Howard, that's all."

"That's not bad at all," Emma agreed. "They're both tall."

"I guess," I replied, but inside I still felt like a big dork. It's like I wasn't feeling like myself lately. I blamed it on the braces. But what I didn't realize was that things were going to get even worse!

CHAPTER 7

More Bad News

On Friday I had to go back to Dr. Payne's to get a mold made of my mouth. My dad was away on a business trip, so there was no decision yet about what kind of braces I was getting. When he called to see how the visit went, he said, "We'll discuss it when I get back, honey." Sometimes I just wish Mom or Dad would make a decision without the other. Anyway, Mom said that since we definitely decided I needed braces, I should get the mold made.

Mom had to work, so Eddie took me. Getting the mold didn't hurt or anything, but it was still pretty horrible. I had to stick my teeth into this disgusting cement stuff that tasted like minty putty. Gross! And I had to do it twice—once for my top teeth, and once for my bottom teeth. When I was done, I rinsed my mouth a million times, but I could still taste the cement.

Luckily, Eddie didn't make any jokes. He stopped and got me a smoothie, so I could try to get the taste out of my mouth, and it helped a little.

Thankfully, the next few days were normal. Nothing exciting happened except for a pop quiz in my science class on Monday. Oh, and Chris Howard talked to me a couple of times in social studies, which was kind of nice. I was hoping maybe things would get back to normal between us.

But then things got weird again on Tuesday, in Mr. K.'s math class. Instead of working in our books like we had been doing, he'd written more equations on the board. I found myself squinting again, but I didn't say anything this time, because I didn't want him to move my seat.

When class started, Mr. K. began talking about equivalent fractions and calling on people in the class. I slumped down in my seat, hoping he wouldn't notice me. But of course he called on me.

"Mia? Can you tell me if these two fractions are equivalent?"

I did my best to squint, but I really couldn't make out the numbers. Instead of giving the wrong answer again, I was just honest. "I can't read the numbers," I said.

A flicker of recognition crossed Mr. K.'s face. "Right! I meant to follow up on this. Randall, please switch places with Mia again. And, Mia, please come talk to me after class."

I moved my seat, and I could see a lot better. I answered the question correctly, and the rest of the class went smoothly. When the bell rang, Katie gave me a sad wave good-bye as she left the room.

I slowly approached Mr. K.'s desk.

"So, Mia, it seems like you're having trouble seeing the board," he said. "Have you been having trouble seeing things far away?"

I hadn't really thought about it until he asked me. But then I remembered that day at the movies with Katie. And how I had mistaken Eddie Rossi for Chris Howard.

"Well, yeah, sometimes," I admitted.

Mr. K. nodded and tapped the wire frame of his eyeglasses. "I was about your age when I got these. It happened the same way. I couldn't see anything written on the blackboard. I kept striking out in baseball. I'm going to shoot your mom an e-mail, recommending that you go see an eye doctor."

Oh great! Another doctor! I thought. Not only

that, but Mr. K. was suggesting I needed glasses. Glasses! It was too cruel to be true. How could I need glasses and braces at the same time?

I didn't want Mr. K. to see that I was upset.

"Okay. Thanks," I said quietly, and then I quickly left the classroom.

A few periods later, at lunch, Katie and I sat down and opened up our lunch bags. Mom had packed me a container of spicy Japanese noodles, one of my favorite lunches. I could tell she was feeling bad for me about the braces.

Wait till she hears about the glasses, I thought. *She'll have to send a personal sushi chef to school with me to make me feel better.*

Alexis and Emma sat down with their hot lunch trays, and that's when Katie asked me, "So, what did Mr. K. want to talk to you about?"

I put down my chopsticks, frowning. "He thinks I need glasses," I said. "Can you believe it? Glasses *and* braces? I might as well forget about my social life."

"First of all, *we're* your social life, and we don't care what you look like," Alexis said. "Second of all, you might be panicking for nothing. Whatever happened to the clear braces?"

"Mom's going to talk to Dad about it when

he drops me off this weekend," I said. "But I don't know what he's going to say."

"Don't leave it up to her," Alexis advised. "You need to work on him. Present your case."

"How?" I asked.

"I'm thinking a PowerPoint presentation," she said. "I can help. Maybe Thursday after school?"

"Oh, definitely," I said gratefully. "Thanks!"

Knowing I had Alexis backing me up on the clear braces made me feel a little better. But that night at dinner, everything fell apart again.

"So, I got an e-mail from Mr. K.," Mom said as we sat around the table eating salmon and broccoli. Dan was at track practice, so it was just Mom and Eddie and me.

"Yeah, I know," I said.

"I've made an appointment with an eye doctor for Monday," Mom told me. She glanced at Eddie. "I'm just surprised I had to hear this from a teacher. Why didn't you tell us you were having trouble seeing the board?"

I honestly didn't know how to answer that. "I don't know. It didn't seem like a big deal."

"It's definitely a big deal, Mia," Mom said. "Your eyesight is very important."

"So how far away can you see?" Eddie asked. He

was sitting across the table from me, and he held up a piece of broccoli. "Can you see this? Is it blurry?"

"Of course I can see it," I snapped.

"Mia, watch your tone," Mom warned.

I sighed. "Sorry," I said, and then I finished my dinner without talking much at all.

But Eddie was still on my case after we finished. I was in the dining room, doing homework, when he appeared in the doorway holding a piece of paper with some letters written on it.

"Can you read these?" he asked.

"Yes!" I said, not looking up from my homework.

"How about from here?" he asked, stepping back into the kitchen.

I was frustrated now. "Are you seriously doing this?"

Mom appeared and placed her hand on Eddie's arm. "Let's leave this up to the eye doctor, okay?"

Eddie nodded. "Sorry, Mia. I'm just worried about you. That's all."

"Don't worry about me," I snapped. "I'm just fine."

But of course I wasn't! I wasn't fine at all.

51

CHAPTER 8

Enhancing My Well-Being

I was glad when the weekend came and I could get away to Manhattan and to my dad. He met me at the train like usual, and that night he surprised me by taking me to see a Broadway show. We had a quick dinner of burgers at a diner first, so we didn't do our usual sushi-restaurant thing we do on Friday nights. I didn't mind, because the show was good, and I had a fun night—with just Dad and me.

The next morning I got my homework done, and then Dad and I went to Greenwich Village to go shopping, and we had lunch at this little restaurant that Dad says has the best sandwiches. As soon as we sat down, I decided to give him my pitch about clear braces. Alexis had prepared a whole computer presentation for me, but I thought Dad would respond better if I made the plea without it. So I had memorized it on the train ride.

"So, as you know, I need braces," I said. "And I am suggesting I get the clear ones instead of the traditional metal ones. Yes, the clear ones are a little more expensive, but I can tell you why they are a better choice for me in the long run."

"Oh, you can?" Dad asked. He looked amused.

"Yes, I can," I said. "The first reason is comfort and safety. Metal braces have wires that can injure your lips and tongue. Second is hygiene. Metal braces can cause tooth decay, because it is difficult to brush and floss around them. But clear braces can be removed for cleaning."

Dad nodded. "Those are good reasons," he said.

"And, finally, the issue at hand is *my* well-being," I went on, trying to remember what Alexis had written. "Middle school and high school are pivotal years for young women. I need self-confidence, and having the clear braces would enhance my well-being."

Dad smiled, and he looked like he was trying not to laugh. "Well, as your dad, I certainly want your well-being to be enhanced," he said. "Is that all?"

"Yes," I said. "I hope you'll take these things into consideration."

"Well, you've given me a lot to think about," he said, still smiling. "I have to discuss this with Mom tomorrow, okay?"

"Okay," I said, but I could tell he looked impressed.

Then the server came by to take our order.

"Do you need another minute?" he asked.

"Yes, please," Dad said, and the waiter nodded and then walked away. Dad gestured to me. "Mia, you should check out the specials board. They always have great stuff there."

He pointed to a chalkboard across the room. I felt like I was right back in Mr. K.'s class. The letters all looked blurry and squiggly.

"Um, I can't really read it," I admitted.

Dad looked alarmed. "What do you mean?"

"Didn't Mom tell you?" I asked. "I might need glasses, too. At least my teacher thinks so."

Dad shook his head. "*Ay, mija,* braces *and* glasses? My poor girl." He took out his cell phone. "Let me text your mom about this. Is she taking you to the eye doctor?"

I nodded. "Monday."

"Good," Dad said.

And then we ate the rest of our meal without talking about braces or glasses, which was nice. My sandwich had cheese and avocado and sprouts on it, and a yummy sauce.

When we were finished eating, Dad looked at his watch. "Great! We'll be just in time for Ethan's play."

I thought I must have heard wrong. "What do you mean 'Ethan's play'?"

"Oh, didn't I tell you?" Dad asked. "Ethan goes to a drama program after school, and they're putting on a little play today. We're meeting Lynne there at two o'clock."

"No, you did not tell me," I insisted. Dad had a habit of doing that lately—not telling me we were doing something with Lynne and Ethan until just before. I think he was worried I would talk him out of it or find some way to back out. He would not be totally wrong.

"Well, anyway, we're going," he said. "Doesn't it sound like fun?"

"A play starring five-year-olds," I said flatly. "Sounds fabulous. What's it called?"

"I think it's something like *The Little Red Hen*," Dad answered.

"Wow. Didn't that win the Tony Award last

year for Best Play?" I said sarcastically.

"Very funny, Mia," Dad said. "Now I trust you'll be nice today. I know *I* would be sweet as a cupcake if I wanted my dad to get me expensive clear braces."

"Okay, okay!" I said quickly. I took his hand. "Let's go see the play!"

We walked a few blocks to Ethan's school and then followed the signs down the stairs, which led to an auditorium-like space in the basement. Lynne was in one of the last rows of folding chairs, waving to us.

We walked up, and Dad gave her a big hug. "Thanks for saving us seats," he said, sitting next to Lynne. I got a seat between Dad and the aisle.

"Hi, Mia," Lynne said. "Thanks for coming."

"You're welcome," I said in my most polite voice.

Lynne had her light brown hair pulled back in a ponytail, and she wore a green long-sleeved sweater over a powder-blue tank top and some sort of puffy, gray, cotton pants. She looked casual but put together. She's not superstylish, like my mom, but not many people are.

Lynne leaned over Dad and asked me some questions about school and stuff, but pretty soon a woman wearing red overalls and bright blue sneakers came out and introduced the play.

"Our drama students have worked very hard on this, and we're all so proud of them," she said. "And now I present to you *The Little Red Hen*."

The play was kind of cute, I guess. One girl played the little red hen, who wanted to bake bread, but none of the farm animals would help her. In the end, she made it herself and then of course all the animals wanted some.

Ethan played a cow. He looked pretty cute in his costume, but I couldn't really make it out too well because we were sitting kind of far from the stage.

Then, during one part of the play, the animals were standing around while the kid playing the pig talked to the little red hen. I heard some people chuckle, and then Lynne gasped.

"Oh no!" she hissed.

I squinted at the stage, but I didn't see anything unusual going on.

"Dad, what's going on?" I whispered.

"It's Ethan," Dad replied. "He's got his finger right up his nose."

"Ewwwww!" I said, trying hard to keep it a whisper. I was glad I couldn't see it. I smiled to myself. Sometimes it's good to have bad eyesight!

CHAPTER 9

Avoiding a Fashion Disaster

On Sunday, Dad took the train with me out to Maple Grove, so he could discuss my braces with Mom. Normally, I'm alone on the train, so it was nice to have company. We laughed a little bit about Ethan's big moment in the play. Part of me was dying to ask Dad if he was planning on marrying Lynne someday, but since he never talked about it, I figured I'd wait and see. I'm still not sure how I'd feel about having Ethan as a little brother.

When the train got to Maple Grove, Mom was waiting for us. It's still a little awkward between Mom and Dad when they meet in person.

"Hello, Sara," Dad said.

"Hello, Alex," Mom replied. They didn't hug or shake hands or anything. And when we got to the car, Mom said, "Mia, you can sit in the front with me." Which meant Dad was in the back. So weird, right?

When we got to the house, Eddie was in super-friendly mode. He shook my dad's hand really hard.

"Good to see you! I've got everything organized for you two here in the dining room," he said, leading Dad hurriedly through the house. "Can I get you something to drink?"

"Water would be great, thanks," Dad said.

Dad sat down at the dining room table, where Eddie had put all the pamphlets and forms about my braces. I went to sit down next to Dad, but Mom shook her head.

"We need some privacy, Mia. We'll let you know when we're done," Mom said.

I groaned a little, but I knew it was no use to argue. Upstairs in my room, I texted Katie.

Mom and Dad r deciding my fate. Clear braces or metal mouth? I typed.

Wishing on my magic unicorn 4 u, Katie typed back.

I laughed. She can be so goofy sometimes.

I didn't have to wait long for Mom to call me back downstairs.

"Well?" I asked, entering the dining room.

Mom looked at Dad and then back at me. "We've decided that you can get the clear braces. They're called aligners, actually. Your dad is going to pay the extra cost, so you owe him a big hug."

Mom didn't even need to say that because I was already hugging Dad as tightly as I could.

"Thankyouthankyouthankyouthankyouthank-youthankyou!" I cried.

"Well, you made such a good case for them," Dad said. "But you have to promise me you'll take good care of them. Like, super extra careful."

I nodded. "I will, I will. I promise. Thanks!"

"And you'll let me know how it goes tomorrow at the eye doctor?" he asked my mom.

"Of course. As soon as she's done we'll call."

Dad came up to see my room, and then we went for a walk to the park, so I could show him a little more of the neighborhood. Then Mom drove us to the train station, and I waved good-bye on the platform while Mom waited in the car. It was all kind of weird saying good-bye to Dad and having Mom stay in the car and everything, but that's how it is now. It's weird but it's normal, I guess.

As soon as Dad left, I texted all my Cupcake friends.

Getting the clear braces! Alexis ur a genius!

Hey what about my lucky unicorn? Katie texted back.

U2! Yaaaaay! ☺☺☺

My good mood last for almost exactly twenty-four hours. That's because the next day, after school, Mom took me for my eye exam. I won't bore you with the details. I had to read charts and look into machines and answer tons of questions. When it was all over, the eye doctor, Dr. Allen, explained that I was nearsighted, which means I can see close-up but not far away. He said I would have to get glasses to wear in class or at the movies—anywhere I needed to see far.

I saved my meltdown until we were back in Mom's car.

"Glasses and braces!" I moaned. "I'm falling apart!"

"You don't have to wear your glasses all the time," Mom pointed out. "Besides, eyeglasses are very fashionable. Most of the biggest clothing designers have a line of eyeglass designs."

"They do?" I asked skeptically.

"Of course. They recognize that glasses are as

much a part of fashion as a dress or a pair of shoes. In fact, some of my clients wear glasses with fake lenses when they want to pull off a certain look."

"I can't believe that," I said.

Mom reached into the backseat and picked up the latest issue of *Elegant* magazine. "Here. Take a look at the ads."

I flipped through the pages, which were mostly filled with ads from the hottest designer lines. In a lot of them, the models were wearing eyeglasses!

"Wow," I said. "I never realized that before."

"See?" Mom said. "Buckle up. I know a great store we can go to."

Mom drove us to Stonebrook, a town that's really close to Maple Grove. The main street of the town has a lot of nice shops there. We found a parking spot in front of a shop called Vision.

Curious, I got out of the car. The shopwindow looked more like an art display than an eyeglasses shop. It featured one female mannequin painted purple and a male mannequin painted turquoise. Each figure was wearing glasses, and nothing else. Orange lights lit up the window with a bright fiery glow.

"Interesting," I remarked, and I saw Mom smile.

Inside, the shop was filled with multiple neat

rows and racks of eyeglasses—more pairs than I could count. It was kind of overwhelming.

"May I help you?" A tall young woman with slick, black hair and a chic purple dress walked up to us.

"My daughter needs eyeglasses," Mom explained. "I have her prescription with us."

The woman smiled. "You came on a great day. We're having a special—buy one pair, get the second half price."

"That's wonderful," Mom said. "Mia really loves fashion, and I thought we could get her one pair that's more classic and another that's a little more playful."

"That's very sensible," the woman said, nodding. She looked at me. "Do you have an idea of what you might want?"

I honestly had no clue. Just like with the braces, I had thought I wouldn't really need them so I hadn't considered what kind of glasses I'd want.

"I'm not sure," I admitted.

Mom put her hands on my shoulders. "With your heart-shaped face, rounder frames might be best. Maybe some frames with a little weight on the bottom. And you've got a warm skin tone, so copper frames would look great. Or you could go with a bold color, like turquoise, maybe."

The saleswoman looked impressed. "Do you do this professionally?"

"She's a stylist," I piped up. "She's even had some famous clients."

"Ah, well, you probably don't need me, then. Feel free to try on whatever you want," the woman said. "In the meantime, to get started I'll pull out a few I think you might like."

So I started trying on glasses, and it was fun! Almost as fun as shoe shopping, but not quite. I tried on pair after pair, posing in the mirror and trying out different faces. I smiled. I pouted. I frowned. I looked surprised. In the end, Mom and I picked out two pairs. The first one, the classic, were simple glasses with thin copper half-rim frames, which had no frames at all on the tops of the lenses. For my fun pair, I chose cute plastic fuchsia ones. Now, I don't have a lot of bright pink in my wardrobe, but that's the point. The fuchsia will give a pop of color to an outfit. I could wear them with blue or black or white or gray, or even green, yellow, or purple.

"It'll take about an hour to get your glasses ready," the woman said. "If you want to wait, you can take them home today."

"Let's wait!" I said anxiously, and I realized that

I was actually kind of excited about the glasses. So Mom and I went to the coffee shop next door. By dinnertime I was home with my brand-new glasses.

Eddie had ordered pizza for us, and he seemed really excited when we got home. "So let me see your exciting new look!" he said.

"One minute," I said, and I ran up to my room. I quickly looked through my closet and picked out outfits to go with my glasses. For the classic one, I put on a plaid skirt and a short-sleeved sweater. Then I put on my glasses and did my best runway walk through the living room.

"Fabulous!" Eddie complimented. "I give them a ten out of ten."

"And now for the funky ones," I said. I ran upstairs again and changed into this purple-and-pink-color-blocked dress I have. I looked in the mirror and had to admit that the fuchsia glasses made the outfit look even cuter than before.

"Mia, that's adorable!" Mom said as I did my runway walk again. "Now why don't we all eat before the pizza gets cold?"

After dinner, when I knew Dad was home from his job, I Skyped him. We do that a lot. Sometimes it's hard to only see him only every two weeks.

I made sure I had on my classic glasses when he logged in.

"Whoa! Who is this sophisticated young woman Skyping me?" Dad asked.

"Do you like them?" I asked him.

"You look beautiful, Mia," he said. "You will always be beautiful to me."

"You have to say that," I accused. "You're my dad."

"But it's true," he said. "Those are very nice glasses."

Between Mom, Dad, and Eddie, I was feeling pretty good about my glasses. But the big test would be tomorrow, when I wore them to school for the first time.

CHAPTER 10

Under My Skin

So how come you're not wearing your glasses?"
Katie asked me the next morning when she got on
the bus.

"I don't need to wear them all the time," I
reminded her. "Just in class, to see the board."

"I'm dying to see them," Katie said.

I started to reach for my backpack, but then I
suddenly felt shy. I mean, we were surrounded by
kids on the bus. I didn't want to draw any extra
attention to myself.

"Math class," I said. "I promise."

Katie dramatically put her hand to her forehead.
"I can't stand the suspense!"

But when we got to math class, I got shy again.
I couldn't bring myself to put my glasses on.

"Come on!" Katie urged.

"Maybe I won't need them," I said. "Not if we're working in our books."

I could tell that Katie wanted to argue with me, but the bell rang. Mr. K. stood up from his desk and went to the board.

"Today I'm going to show you how to convert decimals to percentages," he said, and started writing numbers on the board. Then he turned around. "Mia, do I need to move you to the front row?"

I could tell I was blushing. "Um, no, I have, um . . . I'm good." I took out my glasses to show him.

"Okay. Glad to see that," he said, and then he turned back to the board.

I reluctantly put on my glasses—my classic frames. I could swear that everyone was looking at me, and I felt like I was wearing those giant glasses that clowns wear.

"They look nice," Katie whispered to me.

I was pretty sure she was just trying to make me feel better. But, anyway, I got caught up in what Mr. K. was explaining, and by the time class was over, I almost forgot I was wearing them.

"Did they help?" Katie asked as I put my glasses back in their case.

"Actually, they did," I said. "I could read every-thing perfectly."

"Awesome!" she said with a smile. "And I'm being honest—they really do look nice."

I smiled back. "Thanks." Maybe this wasn't going to be so hard after all.

I put on my glasses during English class next period, and I was able to read all the vocab words on the board. For third period I normally had gym, but our whole gym class was doing health for a couple of weeks—you know, like nutrition and stuff. We met in this classroom next to the gym.

Normally, I like gym because all my Cupcake friends are in it with me. So are the girls in the Best Friends Club. There's Callie Wilson, who used to be Katie's best friend, and who's pretty nice. Bella Kovacs dyes her hair black and is obsessed with vampire movies. Maggie Rodriguez has frizzy hair and is kind of silly and fun. And then there's Olivia Allen. She was new to our school, and I made friends with her—or at least I thought she was my friend. But she was just using me until she found friends she liked better. That's what it felt like to me, anyway. We still talk to each other in the hall and stuff, but we are definitely not friends anymore.

But I have enough of my friends in gym so that having Olivia there doesn't bother me, you know? Things are always easier when your friends are there to back you up.

So when I got to health class, our teacher, Ms. Chen, was setting up the computer projector thingy to show us a film about the human body or something. I put on my glasses so I could see it. We watched the movie, and then Ms. Chen asked us a bunch of questions. When the bell rang I started packing up the glasses again before we headed to lunch.

Suddenly, Olivia was next to me. "Are you a member of the Four Eyes Club now?" she asked, and I flinched. But Olivia wasn't finished. "Don't worry, they don't look that bad. You look like a teacher."

"What do you care what she looks like?" Alexis snapped. She doesn't have a lot of patience for the BFC.

"Okay, chill out! Gosh, can't a person make a comment around here?" Olivia asked. "Anyway, glasses really aren't that bad. They're not as bad as braces, anyway."

I turned pale. Did Olivia know I was getting braces? How could she know? She was really getting under my skin. But she was already walking away.

"I knew this was going to happen," I said as we walked to lunch. "Forget it. I am not wearing these glasses anymore. I'll just keep squinting."

"Mia, you look like you should be in a magazine, seriously," Emma said. "You're gorgeous."

"Yeah, don't listen to her," Katie piped up.

"But does she know I'm getting braces?" I wondered out loud.

"She couldn't," Alexis said. "I think she was just trying to make a jab. A *ridiculous* jab, but just a jab."

I sighed. "I can only imagine what she'll see when I walk in here with braces. This is seriously a disaster."

When we got to the cafeteria, Emma and Alexis went up to the hot food line, and Katie and I went to our table.

"You know," Katie said as she unpacked her lunch. "When I first met you, you were new and everything, but you didn't seem to care what anyone thought. And now you seem to be worried about what everyone is thinking. Why do you care now?"

It was a good question, and I wasn't sure I had an answer. "I don't know," I admitted. "I guess . . .

it's like I knew who I was before, and now I'm this whole new person with glasses and then braces and everything. I'm not the same old Mia anymore."

"Of course you are," Katie insisted. "Just because you have stuff on your face doesn't mean you're not the same inside."

"I guess," I said, and I knew Katie was right. But I was starting to realize something about myself— something that was embarrassing to admit. All my life I had always been, well, kind of cute, you know? Mom always made sure I had really great outfits, and I was always dressed in a cool way. And fashionable. It was easy to feel confident and good about myself when I looked like that on the outside. And so maybe I had to learn how to feel just as confident about the inside of myself, too.

"Just stop caring what people think," Katie advised. "It doesn't matter. I learned that from you."

I felt like hugging her. "What would I do without you?"

"You'd be very, very bored," Katie answered, and we both laughed.

After lunch I had social studies with Katie and all the girls in the BFC, including Olivia. I put on my glasses as soon as I sat down and didn't look at Olivia once. It felt pretty good.

72

Of course, I didn't know what would happen once I had on my braces, too. But for a moment at least, I was happy. I thought my glasses looked nice, and plus, I could actually *see* the board!

CHAPTER 11

A Gooey, Sticky Cupcake Party!

"Welcome to the cupcake party!" Katie shrieked as she opened her front door Friday night.

"You are crazy," I said, shaking my head as she dragged me inside her house.

When we got to her kitchen, Emma and Alexis were already there. On the table were a dozen already baked cupcakes and lots of bowls of toppings.

"Am I late?" I asked. "I thought the meeting was at seven."

"You're not late," Katie replied. "This is a cupcake meeting. It's also a surprise going-away party to your braces-free teeth."

I looked at Emma and Alexis. "What is going on?"

Alexis pointed to the toppings. "Once you get your braces, you won't be able to eat sticky, gooey things. Well, unless you brush your teeth right away. So we have prepared a sticky, gooey feast for you."

Emma held up the first topping bowl like she was a model on a game show. "First, we have delicious gummy worms. So sticky!"

Getting into the spirit, Katie picked up another bowl. "Marshmallow topping. Like glue, but sweet!"

"And perhaps stickiest of all—caramel topping!" Alexis said, pointing to a bowl of golden, creamy goodness.

I couldn't believe it. "You guys are the best!"

Katie picked up a spoon. "Let's do this!"

Katie had made chocolate cupcakes, which were delicious with both the marshmallow and the caramel. We covered the cupcakes with marshmallow topping, some with caramel, and some with both. Then we added gummy worms.

I held up my hands, which were coated with marshmallow and caramel. "This is seriously gross!"

Everyone's hands were the same. Katie looked over at the sink and yelled, "Mom!"

Mrs. Brown came into the kitchen. "Oh, my," she said, looking at the cupcakes. "You are all going to need to brush and floss immediately after you eat these!"

I could tell she was kidding. Even though she is a dentist, she doesn't go around making her guests brush their teeth.

"Can you turn on the faucet for us, please?" Katie asked.

"Gladly!" her mom replied.

We all washed our hands and then settled down to eat our cupcakes. Thankfully, Mrs. Brown poured glasses of milk for us.

"If we didn't have the milk, I think my mouth would be glued shut," I said. "Then I *couldn't* get braces. Hey, maybe that's not a bad idea."

Alexis took a bite of cupcake. "You know, we seriously need to have our meeting. We still don't have an idea for the carnival."

"I'm sorry," I said. "All I can think about these days are glasses and braces."

"I must have spring fever or something," Katie said. "I can't think of anything."

"Maybe spring fever could be a theme," Emma suggested.

Alexis frowned. "I don't know. That kind of sounds like a disease. Not a good way to sell cupcakes."

Emma looked thoughtful. "Okay, it's spring, but we're really celebrating that school will be over soon. So . . . summer? Lemon-yellow sunshine cupcakes?"

"Or butterflies?" Katie suggested. "You know, like we're flying away from school?"

"Hmm. Freedom!" Alexis added.

"My teeth have seen their last days of freedom," I joked. "Tomorrow they'll be going to jail. Clear plastic jail."

Katie took out her phone. "We need a picture of your teeth before they go behind bars. Everybody smile—and show your teeth!"

She leaned her head next to mine and took the picture of all of us smiling. I felt happy, but deep inside, I was really nervous about tomorrow.

I hope this isn't my last smile for a long time! I thought.

CHAPTER 12

The Big Day

$\mathcal{I}$ barely slept that night because I kept having weird dreams about my teeth. In one, they got bigger and bigger, like they were inflating. In another one, my teeth were stuck together and I couldn't open my mouth. Creepy!

When Mom came in to wake me up, I groaned and put my pillow over my head.

"Eddie made a nice breakfast for us," Mom said. "Come down when you're ready, okay? I don't want to be late for Dr. Payne."

I slowly and reluctantly got out of bed, putting on a pair of jeans I found on my floor and the first shirt I pulled out of my drawer. Why should I bother dressing up for something like this? I pulled my hair into a loose ponytail and went downstairs.

The kitchen table was filled with plates of eggs, pancakes, sausage, bacon, and toast. Dan was there, and his plate was piled high, and I wondered how anyone could eat so much.

"Wow, this is a lot of food," I said.

"Well, I wanted to make sure you had a good meal inside you," Eddie replied sheepishly. "In case, you know, your teeth hurt later."

"Thanks for reminding me," I grumbled.

"Mia, Eddie went to a lot of trouble to do something nice for you," Mom scolded.

"Thanks, Eddie," I said, and then I sat down. Everything looked delicious, but I could only eat a small spoonful of scrambled eggs and one piece of bacon, because I was so nervous.

When I was done, I brushed my teeth really well before we left. When we got to Dr. Payne's office, the assistant came out to get us right away. I sat in the chair, and she put the paper bib on me again. Then Dr. Payne walked in smiling.

"Hi, Mia," she said. "I've got your aligners right here."

She opened a case and took out two clear plastic pieces. One was shaped like my top teeth, and the other was shaped like my bottom teeth.

"You already know this, but these are different

79

from metal braces because you can remove them," she explained. "However, you should only remove them to clean your teeth, when you eat, and when you play sports."

I liked the sound of that.

"But first we need to attach the holders to your teeth. That will help keep these in place when they are in your mouth."

I didn't like the sound of that.

It took a long, long time—or at least it seemed like a long time—to glue on all the little pieces. I kept running my tongue over the aligners, and they felt rough. Dr. Payne held up a mirror, and I groaned. They were clear, so maybe far away you couldn't see them, but up close you could definitely see that there was something stuck on my teeth. Gross.

Then Dr. Payne took out these clear-wired things that would attach to the holders.

"I'm going to show you how to clean them, and I'll give you a special case to put them in when you're eating," she went on. "And then we'll try them on, okay?"

"Okay." I nodded. *Maybe this won't be so bad after all,* I thought.

So I watched Dr. Payne demonstrate how to

clean them (with a special soft toothbrush), and then she held up the mirror for me again.

"I'd like you to try putting them in yourself," she said. "It's important that you're comfortable with them."

I nervously picked up the first tray and slid in the aligner. It felt weird—kind of like a glove, but for my teeth. Then I slipped on the bottom one, which felt really tight. Dr. Payne looked at them and then asked me a bunch of questions about how they felt, and she made me bite down and stuff.

"I think you're good to go, Mia," Dr. Payne said with a smile. "Because you're just starting out with these, I'd like to see you in about two weeks, just to make sure you're not having any problems. But if you have any questions in the meantime, you can always call."

"Okay," I said, and it felt weird saying the word. It didn't hurt, really, but I felt like I had a shoe in my mouth or something. Could I ever get used to that? I smiled and looked at myself in the mirror. I reminded myself to thank Alexis for her help in convincing my Dad to get the clear braces. If I didn't smile too much, nobody would even notice them.

Dr. Payne led me out to where my mom was

waiting for me. "Mia will probably experience some soreness in the next day or two. Some pain reliever should help that."

"We'll take care of her. Thank you."

"So how do they feel?" Mom asked me as we walked to the car.

"Strange," I replied, and again, it felt weird to talk.

"Do they hurt?" she asked.

I shook my head. "Not yet. So I was thinking. Maybe we should go to the mall, before I hurt too much to do anything."

Mom smiled. "Yes, that's probably a smart idea."

When we got to the mall, I went right to Icon, to a rack of neon shirts, and picked out a bright yellow one. Now that I didn't have to worry about a metal mouth, I knew I could pull it off. Mom was being supernice to me because of the braces, and she bought it for me.

I was feeling pretty happy. I had a cool new shirt, and my braces were almost invisible. But by the time we got home, my mouth was starting to feel a little sore.

Eddie was waiting by the front door.

"How did it go?" he asked.

I smiled. "They're practically invisible! See?"

"Can't see them at all!" he said. "Do they hurt?"

I nodded. "A little."

"I defrosted some tortilla soup for lunch," he said. "Just in case."

When we sat down to eat the soup, it felt weird having to take out the braces. I put them in the special case Dr. Payne gave me. When I was done, I really didn't want to put them back in, but I knew I had to.

"Maybe you should brush your teeth before you put them in," Mom suggested. "You should do that every time."

"Well, I can't do that at school," I pointed out. "Brush my teeth in the school bathroom? Gross."

"No, of course not," Mom said. "But definitely at home."

So I brushed my teeth and put my braces in again. The soreness was getting worse, so Mom gave me some pain reliever. I went upstairs in my room, put on my headphones, and started drawing in my sketchbook. I like to draw models wearing different outfits, and I found myself drawing eyeglasses on all of them. It looked pretty cool.

The rest of the day was pretty mellow. Mom made a tuna casserole for dinner, which was nice and soft, and then we all rented a movie (except for

Dan, who was out with his friends) and watched it in the living room. I probably could have eaten the popcorn, but I was afraid it might hurt. Or that it would get stuck. It was going to be such a pain to start thinking about what I would eat and how much of it could show up in my teeth.

By the next day, my teeth and jaw were really sore, and I was in a pretty cranky mood. But on the bright side my friends were coming over for a Cupcake meeting.

"Mia, how are you feeling?" Katie asked as soon as she came in the door. "I texted you all day yesterday, but you didn't answer."

"Sorry. I didn't feel like it," I said. "I'm kind of sore."

Katie was staring at my mouth. "Where are they? I can't see them."

I smiled to show her. "They're practically invisible."

The doorbell rang, and I let Alexis and Emma in. They made a fuss over my braces too.

"I owe you one, Alexis," I said. "You saved me from being a metal mouth."

"Maybe you could go into a side business, Alexis," Katie suggested. "Helping people convince their parents to do stuff for them."

Alexis grinned. "That's really not a bad idea. I'm not sure how to market it, but it's worth exploring." She started to quickly type a note into her phone.

It was a nice day, so we went outside on our back deck to have our meeting. Earlier, I'd helped Mom make some iced tea mixed in with lemonade. We sat around the table, under the umbrella, and sipped our beverages as we talked.

"So, we still need a theme for the carnival cupcakes," Alexis began.

"I know!" Katie said. "I don't know why I'm so stuck. Usually we agree much faster than this. What's wrong with butterflies again?"

"Nothing, really, except that we were trying to think of something more summery," Alexis reminded us.

"Then how about fireflies?" Emma suggested.

"That would be so cute," I agreed. "But it might take a lot of work to make them out of fondant or candy or whatever, especially if we have to make a few hundred cupcakes. Fireflies can be pretty detailed."

Alexis nodded. "What else makes summer special? Staying up late?"

"Fireworks?" Katie added. "Sunshine?"

An idea was forming in the back of my mind. "When I think of summer, I think of how things are, like, easier, you know? You don't have to wear a coat or put on a hat or mittens or even a sweater. You can just throw on shorts, a tank top, and flip-flops and you're good to go."

Emma was nodding. "Right. Most mornings I don't even blow-dry my hair. I just put it up wet in a ponytail."

"You mean, like, 'Come as You Are'?" Alexis asked.

"Exactly. 'Come as You Are,'" I said.

"It's good," Katie said thoughtfully. "But how do you turn that into a cupcake?"

Alexis sighed. "I declare us officially stumped. But we *have* to come up with something at our next meeting. How does Thursday work for everyone?"

We all quickly checked our schedules and agreed that Thursday was good.

"Great. We'll meet at my house," Alexis said. Then we just hung out for a while in the sunshine, goofing around. It was kind of nice not to have to do anything but hang out.

After my friends left, I took out my sketchbook and tried to come up with a cool cupcake design. But I couldn't think of anything because I was stressing about what would happen tomorrow. I would be debuting my braces at school for the first time. Would anyone notice?

CHAPTER 13

It *Is* a Big Deal!

"Mia, hurry up!" Mom yelled up the stairs. "You're going to miss the bus!"

"But I'm not ready yet!" I yelled, fighting back tears.

It had been a terrible morning. My jaw had been throbbing all night, and I didn't sleep well. I could only get down some oatmeal for breakfast, and then I had to brush my teeth, and then clean the braces and then put them back in, which took forever.

Then I went to get dressed, and I planned to wear my new neon yellow top and some leggings. The outfit looked great and didn't clash with my invisible braces at all. But then I remembered my glasses. I tried on my classic pair, and the copper didn't look that great with the yellow. Then I put on the fuchsia glasses, which might have looked good with, say, a light, lemony yellow, but they looked just awful with the new top. I sighed and got undressed. Normally, I pick out my outfit the night before, but I didn't last night and I didn't have a backup plan.

I put on a short denim skirt with a blue top, but then I couldn't find my blue ballet flats to go with it. I tried on my black flats, but they didn't go with the outfit at all. So I dug through my closet until I found a short-sleeved, black top with ruffled sleeves and tried that on. It looked good with the skirt and the flats. Then I tried my classic glasses, and they looked okay. But that was a lot of work.

So much for "Come as You Are," I thought glumly.

Then I reviewed my plan in my head: Nobody knew about the braces except my friends. When I opened my mouth, it was hard to tell I was wearing braces, even though I still felt like I was chewing on a shoe. So nobody had to know I was wearing braces, just as long as I was cool about it.

"Okay. You can do this," I told my reflection.

By the time I got downstairs, Mom was standing by the front door, holding her car keys and looking annoyed. I missed the bus.

"I'll have to drive you," she said. "So please get in the car right now, because I have a conference call in a half hour."

I grabbed my backpack and followed her outside without saying a word. The whole way to school she was lecturing me about being on time.

"I understand this is a new routine for you, Mia, so maybe you need extra time in the morning," she said. "I can wake you up fifteen minutes earlier. Maybe your bedtime should be earlier, too."

"But that's not fair!" I argued.

"Mia, it's not up for discussion," Mom said firmly.

I sulked the whole way to school. Not only did I have to wear glasses and braces, but I now also had to go to bed earlier. What *else* could go wrong?

When I got to school, I found Katie on the steps, talking with Sophie and Lucy. Katie looked relieved to see me and came running up.

"Are you okay?" she asked. "I thought maybe you were staying home because your mouth hurts from your braces."

"Shhh," I said, leading her away by the arm. "I don't want anybody to know, okay?"

Katie shrugged. "Okay. I don't see what the big deal is, though. Lots of kids have braces, and most of them have the metal ones that you can see."

"Well, it's a big deal to me," I replied.

"Okay, okay!" Katie said. She pretended to lock her mouth with a key. "My lips are sealed."

"How can they be sealed if you just said that?" I teased, and we started laughing. I quickly covered up my mouth with my hand, and Katie rolled her eyes.

"Mia, you can't tell, I swear!" Katie insisted.

"Well, I'm not taking any chances," I replied.

My plan went pretty well that morning. I made sure not to smile or open my mouth wide, and nobody noticed I had in my braces, not even my teachers. I was playing it cool with my glasses, too. I kept them in my backpack until I absolutely needed to look at the board. Then I quickly slipped them on and took them off again when I was done.

That's what I did in math, and I caught Katie giving me a weird look. She just didn't understand my plan.

Right now, you might be agreeing with Katie. I mean, my braces were invisible, and I only had to wear my glasses sometimes. No big deal, right? But to me, it really was. I can't explain it. I just felt like if I didn't look perfect all the time, everybody would stare at me or make fun of me. And it wasn't even about looking perfect. It was about looking like me. I was used to looking a certain way. Now all of a sudden I was wearing glasses and my teeth were covered in brace stuff, and I just don't look the same. It was a lot to get used to all at once.

When it came time for lunch, I opened my lunch bag. Mom had packed me some yogurt and a container with some nice, soft pasta salad in it. I was about to start eating when I remembered that I had to take out my braces, but I didn't have a plan for that. Wouldn't everyone see me? I thought about going into the restroom, but it was always crowded at lunchtime.

Then I had an idea. I took my social studies book out of my backpack and propped it up on the table in front of me. I opened it up, so that it was sort of shielding my face on all sides. Then I quickly slipped out the braces, put them in the container, and then lowered the book.

That's when I noticed Katie, Alexis, and Emma staring at me.

"Uh, hi," I said awkwardly.

"What was that all about?" Alexis asked.

"I have to take out my braces when I eat," I explained. "But I don't want anybody to see me."

"Why not?" Emma asked.

Katie answered for me. "She doesn't want anyone to know she has braces."

"But they're invisible," Alexis pointed out.

"Not entirely," I argued. "They're shiny and big. See?"

I smiled, and then quickly closed my mouth. "Listen, it's not just about the braces. It's braces and glasses at the same time. Ugh!"

"But the braces are temporary, and besides, nobody cares what you look like," Katie said. "And even if *you* care what you look like, you look great. Like the same old Mia."

"Right," agreed Emma. "You look terrific."

"Spectacular," Alexis added.

"Thanks, guys," I said. My friends were being so nice that it was hard to stay in a bad mood. "I don't know what I would do without you."

"So maybe you can just relax a little," Katie suggested.

"I'll try," I promised. "But if anybody makes fun of me, it's on you guys!"

CHAPTER 14

We Finally Have a Theme!

$\mathcal{F}$or the next few days I mostly took my friends' advice. I put my glasses on when I got to class, and nobody said anything. And I kept quiet about my braces, and nobody said anything about them either. I stopped hiding a book in front of me when I took them out at lunch. I just acted normal, and that seemed to work out pretty well.

At lunch on Thursday we were talking about our Cupcake Club meeting.

"So, are we all walking to your house after school, Alexis?" I asked.

"If it's okay with you, can we have the meeting at four?" Alexis asked. "I have to, um, do something after school."

That was a little bit weird, because most times

we met right after school. Now I'd have to take the bus all the way home and then find somebody to drive me to Alexis's house. I looked at Katie.

"Can I go to your house from the bus, so we can go together?" I asked.

Katie and Alexis exchanged a strange look, and then Katie said, "Um, no, my mom doesn't want me to have anybody over when she's not there."

That didn't make sense. "But we've done that before," I pointed out.

Katie shrugged. "I don't know. She must be going through a 'strict' phase. You know how she can get."

Katie's mom did have some unusual rules, so I didn't think too much of it. Plus, Mom is usually home in the afternoon, so I knew she could drive me.

So at four o'clock Mom dropped me off at Alexis's house. The outside of the house is just as neat as it is on the inside. The bushes by the front door are always trimmed into perfect globe shapes, and I swear the lawn never looks like it grows—the grass is always the same height.

When I knocked on the door, Alexis answered from inside.

"Just come in!"

I obeyed and followed the sound of her voice to the kitchen. Alexis, Emma, and Katie were all sitting around the kitchen table, and each one of them was wearing glasses!

I started laughing. "Oh my gosh! What did you guys do?"

"We're supporting you!" Emma said.

"If you're going to be Four Eyes, then we're all Four Eyes!" Alexis added proudly.

"Don't we look great?" Katie asked. "We got reading glasses at the dollar store and took the lenses out."

I was really touched. And more than that, I was amazed by how cute my friends looked. They didn't look dorky or weird at all.

"You guys are the best," I said, sitting down with them. "And you all look amazing too!"

"So do you when you wear *your* glasses," Katie said. "I hope you believe us now."

"I do," I said, although I wasn't sure if I believed it 100 percent yet. "But, hey, don't we have a cupcake job to plan? We only have, like, a week before we start baking."

"You sound like me," Alexis joked. "And you're right. We need a plan, like, right now. I baked some cupcakes last night. Plus, Katie brought all the leftover supplies from our last few jobs."

Alexis had neatly set up everything on the kitchen counter. I looked over and saw a tray of vanilla cupcakes, along with sprinkles, edible glitter, chocolate chips, gummy worms, coconut, and a whole bunch of other stuff.

"I was thinking," Katie said. "Maybe we don't need all that stuff. If this is supposed to be 'Come as You Are,' then maybe our cupcakes should be, like, naked. No frosting, no decorations. Just plain."

We all started giggling at that. "Naked cupcakes? Principal LaCosta would throw us out of the carnival if we did that," I said.

"Plus, they wouldn't be yummy," Emma said.

"And they might be boring," Alexis added.

Katie got up and brought the tray of "naked" cupcakes to the table. Then she picked one up and started talking in the voice of a cupcake (which was sort of high-pitched, which I guess is how Katie thinks a cupcake would sound if it could talk).

"I'm not boring! I'm naked! I'm ready for summer sunbathing!" Katie said.

We were all cracking up now. Emma picked one up that had puffed up higher on one side than the other. "Look at me! I'm lopsided!"

I grabbed one that was smaller than the others.

"I'm tiny, but I'm still delicious!" I said in my best impersonation of Katie's cupcake voice.

"See?" Katie said. "Not boring at all."

"That's only if we do cupcake voices for the whole carnival," Alexis pointed out. "And I'm not sure I have that in me."

"But it's cool the way all the cupcakes are different and unique," I said, finally figuring it out. "So maybe that's what we do. We have to make about a hundred cupcakes, right? So let's do them in a bunch of different flavors. Then each one could have a different icing and topping. I mean, like mixing them up. Just so each one is unique."

"I *love* that!" Emma cried. "That will be so much fun!"

"Yay!" Katie agreed. "But we'll have to narrow down how many flavors and icings we do, so we don't go crazy. And I think we have enough extra toppings that we won't have to buy new stuff, so that's good for our budget, right?"

Alexis nodded. "That's *great* for our budget. This is a terrific idea."

I grabbed a cupcake. "Let's play around with the dozen we have here to see how they could look. Is there any icing?"

"I made a batch of vanilla," Alexis said. "And we

could always add food coloring to it."

"Perfect!" I said. "Let's decorate some and see how they look."

We brought the icing and the toppings onto the kitchen table and started decorating our practice cupcakes. I used a paper cup to make a small batch of pale orange frosting for one cupcake. I used a black icing tube to draw hair that sort of looked like mine. Then I made a mouth with big teeth out of tiny white candies.

"Alexis, do you have any cereal?" I asked.

"In the cabinet to the right of the sink."

I found a box of round cereal with a hole in the middle of each piece, which was just what I needed. I added them as the eyes of the cupcake. Then I added some more details with the icing tube. When I was done, I held it up.

"Look!" I said. "It's me with glasses and braces!"

That made everyone laugh. I made another one with glitter and jelly beans, and for my third one I designed an intricate pattern with a red icing tube over purple icing. It looked pretty cool.

When we were done, we put our twelve cupcakes together. Katie had made glitter rainbows on hers. Emma's had pink hearts all over them. Alexis made cool geometric designs with candy. They all looked different, but still worked great together as a group.

"This is awesome," Alexis said, standing back to admire them. "What I love about this is that there will be something for everyone at the carnival."

"People can find their cupcake soul mate," Katie said.

"It might take us a long time to do one hundred," I realized. "We might want to simplify our designs a little bit."

"We can bake on Thursday and decorate on Friday," Alexis suggested.

"Let's do it at my house this time," Katie offered. "We have lots of extra decorating stuff in our closets, and Mom won't mind if we use it."

Alexis held up a cupcake. "Here's to our not-naked cupcakes!" she cried, and we all clinked together our cupcakes.

CHAPTER 15

Two Surprising Comments

Thanks to my friends, I was finally starting to feel better about my glasses. Then something happened at school the next day that really surprised me.

It happened after health class, on the way to lunch. In class, I had put on my glasses as soon as I sat down, because I had pretty much gotten into the habit of doing that. Across the room, I saw Callie of the BFC kind of staring at me, and I felt a little nervous. Was she going to call me Four Eyes too?

I didn't really think she would, because Callie is the nicest member of the BFC. There was a time when I hung out with them for a little while, and Callie almost never said anything mean about anybody when the girls were gossiping. Sometimes I still hang out with the BFC if I run into them in the mall when I'm clothes shopping (which is a lot, as you can tell). Katie *hates* clothes shopping, so I don't feel bad about hanging out with them, and besides, she understands.

But Callie's staring made me nervous—you never know with those BFC girls. So I tensed up a little bit when she walked up to me after class. I was heading to lunch with Katie, like always.

"Hi, Mia," she said. "Hi, Katie."

"Hi," Katie replied, a little coolly. (Things are still kind of awkward between them, because they're not best friends anymore.)

"Mia, I wanted to talk to you about your glasses," Callie said, and I noticed she was looking around, like she didn't want anyone to hear her. "You look so cool in yours! I wish I could pull them off, but I don't think glasses would look good on me, so I wear contact lenses."

"No way," Katie interrupted. "When did you get those?"

"Last year," Callie said. "They're okay, but it creeps me out to take them in and out. I think it would be much easier to wear glasses all the time. Where did you get yours? They look so awesome on you."

"My mom helped me," I admitted. "She knows

all about what shapes and colors work best for your face and skin tone. We went to this shop in Stonebrook. It's called Vision."

"Thanks. Maybe I'll tell my mom."

Then I had an idea. "You know, I could go with you if you want. I remember all that stuff my mom told me. And the saleswoman knows a lot too, so she could help."

"Oh my gosh, that would be so awesome!" Callie said, excited. "Could we go this weekend, maybe?"

"I'm with my dad this weekend," I replied. "Maybe Monday after school?"

"I'll ask my mom and text you," Callie said. "Thank you so much!"

Then she hurried ahead to catch up with the BFC.

"That's amazing," I said. "Not only did she not call me Four Eyes, but she actually *wants* to get glasses."

"It's really nice of you to help her," Katie said, and I could tell she wasn't jealous at all. "You could become a stylist, just like your mom."

"Or a fashion designer," I said, because that is one of my goals. "But being a stylist would be cool, too."

Right then I decided I wasn't going to be embarrassed about my glasses ever again. It wasn't just Callie that did it; it was everyone who had helped me. And I realized it was a relief not to care about it anymore!

I brought both pairs of glasses with me to my dad's for the weekend, so I could coordinate them with my outfits. On Friday night we had our traditional sushi dinner, and I made sure to ask Dad if we were going to see Lynne and Ethan that weekend. He said there was a concert in the park that might be fun, and he thought we could all go together.

That sounded okay to me. But when I woke up Saturday morning, the sky was gray. It was still cloudy when Lynne and Ethan came over that afternoon.

"Are you sure we should go?" Lynne asked worriedly. "It looks like it might rain."

"The forecast says that the rain is going to hold off until early evening," Dad reported, and right at the end of his sentence we heard a loud clap of thunder. I walked to the window, and sheets of rain were splashing against the glass.

"Um, I think the forecast is wrong," I said.

"That's okay," Lynne said. "Ethan and I can go home and watch a video."

"Nonsense! You can't go out in this," Dad insisted. "Stay here, and we can rent a movie or something."

He kneeled down to talk to Ethan. "Would you like that? What movie should we rent?"

"I don't want to see a movie," Ethan said, pouting. "I want to play in Mia's room!"

Dad later told me that the look on my face was like I had seen an alien crashing through the ceiling. I must have looked horrified. Making sure only Dad could see me, I started shaking my head. No way did I want Ethan in my room!

But Dad wasn't having it. "I'm sure Mia wouldn't mind showing you her room, would you, Mia?"

Yes, I would! Very much! I wanted to scream. But I didn't want to embarrass Dad or make Lynne feel bad.

"Sure," I said, my voice tight. "Come on, Ethan."

I opened the door to my room, which Dad helped me decorate exactly the way I wanted when he got this apartment. It's Parisian chic— pale pink walls with black and white accents, and a wrought iron headboard for my bed, and I even have a vanity where I can sit and do my hair in the morning. But Ethan did not appreciate my Parisian chic decor at all.

"Where are your toys?" he asked, looking around. "You don't have any toys."

"No," I said. "I'm older than you are. I don't have toys anymore."

But Ethan walked around, looking under and on top of things, determined to find some toys.

"I have dinosaur toys," he informed me. "Dinosaur toys are awesome."

"Well, I don't have any of those," I replied. "Sorry. Maybe we should go back into the living room and watch a movie."

Then he pulled a tin of colored pencils out of my open backpack. "Can we color?" he asked me.

"Not with those!" I said, quickly grabbing them from him. "I use them for my fashion sketches."

Ethan took out my sketchbook. "In here?" he asked, and he started flipping through the pages before I got it back from him. "These are just dresses. Can't you draw dinosaurs?"

"Of course I can draw dinosaurs," I said, feeling a little defensive. I wasn't going to let a little kid insult my drawing skills. I took the sketchbook from him. "What's your favorite dinosaur?"

"Apatosaurus," he said without hesitating. "I bet

you can't draw it. It's going to be too hard."

"Can too," I shot back. "I just need some reference, that's all."

"What's 'reference'?" Ethan asked.

I took out my phone and searched for "apatosaurus." A picture of a giant dinosaur with a long neck and tail popped up. "See? I need to look at a picture of something, so I'll know how to draw it. That's what 'reference' means."

Ethan nodded. "Draw it!"

I started to sketch, and Ethan just watched me, as quiet as could be. When I finished, I showed him.

"That's really good," he said. "Can I draw something?"

I thought for a minute, and then I remembered I still had crayons and paper in my desk from when I made decorations for the twins' music party. I gave them to Ethan and he started to draw. I realized I wanted to draw another dinosaur.

"What other dinosaurs do you like?" I asked.

"Mmm . . . triceratops," Ethan answered.

I knew that one. That's the one with the three horns on its head. I drew a triceratops, and then for fun I drew Ethan riding on it.

"How about this one?" I asked him.

His face lit up. "Is that me?"

I nodded. "Yes. What do you think?"

Ethan thought for a minute. "Put balloons on it," he ordered, and so I drew some balloons tied to the dinosaur's tail. This made Ethan crack up so hard, I thought he was going to hurt himself. Pretty soon I was laughing too.

Dad stuck his head in the room. He looked really surprised and really happy that we were getting along. "Everything okay in here?" he asked, looking around. I think he thought maybe I'd tied up Ethan and put him in the closet.

"We're drawing," I said, holding up my pictures.

"Mia's good at drawing," said Ethan appreciatively.

"Mia's great at drawing," Dad agreed with a huge smile. "We ordered some pizza. Why don't you guys come join us?"

"Pizza!" yelled Ethan and went charging into the kitchen.

So we all had pizza, and then it was time for Lynne and Ethan to leave.

"I don't want to go," Ethan said, tearing up. "I don't want to leave Mia's house."

Mia's house. It was kind of cute. I had always thought of this as Dad's house, mostly because I don't live here all the time. But I guess it was my house too. I had to give Ethan a big hug.

"I'll be back in two weeks," I said. "Maybe we can draw pictures again."

"Of dinosaurs?" Ethan asked.

"Sure!" I said.

Ethan thought a minute. "How about whales?"

"Um . . . sure," I said. "I can draw whales."

Ethan gave me a hug and a big grin.

When they left, Dad turned to me with a smile on his face. "Wow, Mia, you really made an impression on Ethan."

I shrugged. I didn't want Dad to think I was totally cool with the idea of being Ethan's big sister or whatever.

"I guess he can be pretty cute when he's not picking his nose," I said, and left it at that.

CHAPTER 16

Utter Humiliation!

Callie and I went shopping for glasses for her on Monday, along with her mom. It was really fun. She tried on dozens of glasses, and she ended up picking out two pairs, just like I had: a classic pair with silver metal frames and a funky pair with clear frames and little rhinestones in the corners.

"I can't wait to wear them to school!" Callie said on the ride home. "It's going to be such a relief not to have to put those contacts in and out."

"You're going to look great!" I told her, and then I realized that's what everyone had been saying to me, and I never believed them. But I knew I wasn't lying to Callie, because she did look super-cute!

When Katie and I got off the bus the next

day, we saw Callie and the BFC girls talking on the front steps. Callie was wearing her new classic glasses, and she was working them. The silver frames looked really pretty with her curly blond hair and blue eyes, and she had on these cute denim shorts with a lacy white top and pink flats. I loved her whole look.

"Callie, your glasses look really nice," Katie remarked as we walked past.

"Duh. She doesn't need you to tell her that," Olivia said, rolling her eyes. But Callie ignored her.

"Thanks, Katie," Callie said. "I owe it all to Mia. She helped me pick out the best ones."

I could see Olivia fume when Callie said that. Olivia likes to think she's a fashion maven.

"No problem!" I said breezily, and then Katie and I walked away. Katie gave me a knowing look and giggled.

I was feeling like the old Mia again. My glasses were a cool fashion accessory. Nobody knew I had braces. The worst was behind me—or so I thought.

When my friends and I talk about the incident today, I call it "The Big Embarrassment." I don't think I will ever forget what happened, not as long as I live.

See, my teeth weren't hurting anymore, so Mom

had started packing me lunches that I could chew. So for lunch that day she'd packed a spinach salad with chicken on top and some wheat crackers on the side. Yum, right?

I took off my braces to eat, and I was having a great time at lunch. Alexis was telling us a funny story about her older sister, Dylan, and how she had freaked out before getting ready for a party Saturday night. Then I remembered I'd forgotten to tell everyone about what Ethan did during the play.

"Poor Ethan!" Alexis said. "Was everyone laughing at him?"

"It wasn't too bad," I reported. "He didn't seem to notice, anyway."

"He sounds kind of cute," Emma said. "Do you think he's going to be your little brother?"

"I don't know," I said, holding up my hands. "Hey, I just got used to braces and glasses. One major change at a time."

I slipped my braces back on, then picked up the napkins and stuff left over from my lunch. "Be right back," I said, and then I headed over to the trash can.

As I walked there, Chris Howard got up from his table and approached me. My heart started to pound a little faster. This was more than just talking in class.

"Mia, wasn't that social studies test yesterday the worst?" he asked. "I mean, it was, like, all essay questions!"

"Totally," I agreed, giving him a big smile. "It's like Mrs. Kratzer does it just to torture us."

"I think I did okay, though," he said. "I bet you got an A. You always know all the answers when she calls on you."

"Well, so do you," I replied truthfully. Chris is not only cute, but he's pretty smart.

Hey, Chris is flirting with you—and you're flirting back! a little voice inside me chirped, and I realized I was having fun.

"Yeah, I actually had to use my extra pen during that class," I said. "I wrote so much that my first pen ran out of ink!"

"That is insane," Chris said, shaking his head, and we both laughed.

Just then, Olivia walked past us. She stopped when she saw me.

"Oh my gosh, Mia, what's that in your mouth?" she asked, stepping closer to me.

I immediately covered my mouth with my hand. "What do you mean?"

"There's, like, all this stuff in your teeth," Olivia said. "Oh, no way. Do you have braces?"

I didn't answer her. I didn't even say good-bye to Chris. I just quickly tossed my trash in the garbage and then ran back to the table. I turned to Katie and opened my mouth.

"Katie, do my braces look weird or something?" I asked.

Katie's eyes got wide. "I think you got a bunch of spinach stuck up in there. You'd better go to the bathroom."

I quickly ran to the girls' room, with Katie right behind me. When I looked in the mirror, I saw that my top teeth were green! I must have gotten some spinach in my teeth, and then when I slipped the braces on, it got all flattened out and stuck.

"I look like a monster!" I shrieked, tearing out my top braces tray. I rinsed it out and then started to rinse the spinach out of my mouth.

"It wasn't so bad," Katie offered.

"Are you kidding?" I wailed. "I was talking to Chris for, like, five minutes! He had to have noticed. And then Olivia said something, so I know for sure that *she* knows."

"So what? You don't care what Olivia thinks," Katie reminded me.

I knew she was right. "I guess so. But I care what Chris thinks."

Katie shook her head. "Don't let it bother you. Chris likes you whether you have stuff stuck in your teeth or not."

But I felt completely humiliated. "Can you please get my backpack? I'm going to stay in here until the bell rings."

Katie sighed. "Okay. But you're being silly."

As soon as Katie left, I felt kind of dumb hiding out in the bathroom, but when I thought about going out and facing Chris, I just couldn't do it. While I waited, I decided to make a list on my phone, so that it would never happen again.

1. No food that can get stuck in teeth. Soft food and liquids only.
2. No food with color.
3. No smiling, ever.

Yes, it was drastic. But I was determined that I was never, ever going to be embarrassed like that again.

For the rest of the day, I walked around without smiling or opening my mouth. I talked in class only when I was called on. I didn't relax until soccer practice after school, when I was allowed to take out my braces.

That night at dinner, Eddie made spaghetti with tomato sauce.

"It's Eddie Spaghetti night!" he joked, like he always does.

I was about to dig in when I remembered my rules, and I stopped. The tomato sauce was bright red.

"Is everything okay?" Mom asked, watching me.

I kept thinking. The spaghetti smelled delicious, and I could brush my teeth right after, so I decided it was okay to eat. Lunch, tomorrow, was another matter.

"Mom, can I have vanilla yogurt for lunch tomorrow?" I asked.

Mom looked concerned. "Are your teeth still hurting, honey?"

"A little," I lied. "Would that be okay?"

Mom nodded. "I'll run out and get some after dinner."

I felt a little guilty making Mom run out like that, but not too guilty. After what happened with Chris, I was not going to take any chances!

CHAPTER 17

My Crazy Friends

For the next couple of days I got really good at sticking to my list. I made sure not to smile or open my mouth when I laughed. I stayed quiet in class, and I didn't even talk much at lunch.

At lunch on the first day I vowed to keep to my list, Katie, Alexis, and Emma spent the whole time trying to convince me that things weren't so bad.

"I saw Chris smiling at you all during social studies," Katie said.

"He's probably remembering my giant green teeth and laughing," I said glumly.

"If he noticed, he would have said something," Alexis pointed out, trying to use logic. "You should just go up and talk to him today like nothing's wrong."

"If anything, he probably thinks it's weird you ran away from him like that," Emma said.

I groaned and put my head on the table. "Oh great! I totally forgot I did that. That's even *more* embarrassing!"

On Thursday at lunch, I noticed that my friends did not talk about my teeth or my whole not-smiling thing at all. Alexis started a Cupcake Club meeting instead.

"So, we're making chocolate, vanilla, and strawberry cupcakes, right?" she asked. "Katie, did you get all the ingredients?"

Katie nodded. "Mom and I went shopping last night. We're all set."

"Give me the receipt, so you can be reimbursed," Alexis said.

"Cool," Katie said. "Mom said we could do it at five, when she gets home. She'll order Chinese food for us."

We all agreed that sounded good. Mom dropped me off at Katie's right at five.

"Are you going to be okay eating the Chinese food?" Mom asked. "Most of it's soft, right?"

"I guess I'll be okay," I replied. I was glad Mom was worried about me. Most of the time it was annoying, but at times like these, it felt good that she cared so much about me. I gave her a hug. "We're just baking tonight, so we should be done around eight."

"Text me," Mom said, and then I got out of the car.

When I rang the bell, Katie called to me from inside the house.

"Door's open!"

I walked inside, curious. It kind of reminded me of the time when they all surprised me by wearing glasses. And when I got into the kitchen, Alexis and Emma were already there. But nobody had on glasses. They all looked exactly the same as usual.

The weird thing was that nobody was saying anything.

"What's up?" I asked.

The girls slowly opened their mouths at the same time. Each one of them had stuff stuck in her teeth! Katie had rainbow sprinkles and icing, Emma had gummy bears, and Alexis had two long strands of licorice hanging down from her two front teeth.

I started laughing. "Get out! You guys are too much."

"Do you like us any less?" Katie asked.

I shook my head. If anything, I loved them even more.

119

"Exactly!" Katie said. "So stop moping around. And start smiling again, please. We miss the old Mia."

Katie looked so funny when she talked. "It's hard to take you seriously when you look like Rainbow Brite," I said, giggling like crazy.

"I don't understand what's so funny," Alexis joked as the licorice wiggled back and forth as she talked.

"Yeah, we look perfectly normal," Emma said, giving me a big, wide, gummy bear–filled smile.

"Okay, okay, I promise!" I said. "Please get that stuff out of your teeth. It's too weird."

"I don't know, I kind of like this look," Katie joked. "Although if my mother sees this, she'll have me brushing my teeth ten times a day from now on."

Soon my friends had their normal teeth back, and we got to work baking the cupcakes. We baked four dozen vanilla cupcakes, three dozen chocolate cupcakes, and two dozen strawberry cupcakes. I know that sounds like a lot, but we're used to big jobs by now. And when the oven was filled with baking cupcakes, and we had more pans of cupcakes ready to go, we sat down and ate our Chinese food.

Mrs. Brown had ordered a bunch of stuff, including wonton soup, which I love. It's meat-filled dumplings floating in a broth with green onions. For a second I thought about skipping it, so I wouldn't get green onions stuck in my teeth. And then a picture of Alexis and her licorice teeth popped into my head.

I poured myself a bowl and took a nice, big slurp with a big piece of green onion in it. Sure, it might get stuck in my teeth, but thanks to my friends, I didn't care one bit.

CHAPTER 18

You're Not Going to Believe This . . .

The next day we were supposed to decorate cupcakes at Katie's again, but first I had an appointment with Dr. Payne—just a quick checkup to make sure everything was okay.

When we got to her office, there was already another kid sitting there waiting. Mom frowned.

"I guess she's a little backed up," Mom said after she signed me in. "I need to go make a call. Sit tight, and I'll be right back."

Mom stepped into the hallway, and I sat back on the comfy light blue couch and sighed. There were a bunch of magazines on the coffee table, and I noticed the latest copy of *Teen Style* poking out from the pile. I picked it up and started flipping through it.

At least I don't need glasses to read, I thought gratefully.

"Hey, Mia."

I looked up to see Chris Howard standing over me. A woman I guessed was his mom was talking to the receptionist at the front desk.

"Oh, hey," I said.

Chris sat down next to me. "Are you getting braces too?" he asked.

"I, um, I already have them," I admitted.

"No way!" Chris said. "I never noticed. Are they invisible or something?"

Hadn't noticed? Was he kidding? So Chris hadn't noticed the spinach after all. Unbelievable. I opened my mouth to show him.

"Yeah. I got the invisible ones, so you can't really see them," I explained.

"That is so cool," Chris said. "I asked Dr. Payne about those, but she said they won't work on my kind of teeth. I guess I have mutant teeth or something."

I laughed. "Your teeth look perfectly normal to me."

"I wish," Chris said, and I could tell he looked nervous. "So do those clear ones hurt?"

"A little, at first. But I heard it's the same with

123

metal ones. They hurt at first, and you can get them adjusted, but then most of the time you don't feel them."

"That's what Dr. Payne said, but I didn't believe her," Chris confessed.

I remembered what Emma's brother Sam had said. "Even when it hurts, it's not so bad, because you can ask for ice cream for dinner," I told him.

Chris grinned. "That doesn't sound too bad." He took a deep breath. "Okay, maybe I can do this."

Chris's mom and my mom came over and then sat by us at the same time. Chris's mom is short, which was kind of funny because Chris is so tall. But I noticed they had the same green eyes.

"Mom, this is my friend Mia," Chris said.

"I remember Mia," Mrs. Howard said, smiling at me. "You two went to the pep rally dance together, right?"

Chris and I both nodded.

"It's nice to meet you," Mom said, smiling and shaking Mrs. Howard's hand.

"You too," she replied. "I'm very glad we ran into Mia today. I couldn't help overhearing their conversation. Chris was nervous, but Mia has been so helpful and reassuring. Thank you, Mia."

I think I blushed a little, and so did Chris.

"Um, you're welcome," I said, a little shyly.

From the corners of my eyes, I could see our moms smiling at each other.

Aaaagh! They think we're cute together! I thought, and then, thankfully, the receptionist called my name.

The appointment was really fast. Dr. Payne said everything looked good, and I didn't have to come back for six weeks. As we left, I waved good-bye to Chris, and he smiled at me.

"Good luck," I called. "It will be fine."

"Thanks!" he said, but he still looked a little nervous. "Ice cream and milk shakes, right?"

"Yes!" I said. "For breakfast, lunch, and dinner!"

He grinned. "Cool. We can have ice cream together for lunch!"

Did he just say that? He did!

"Awesome!" I said, because I couldn't think of anything else to say. I kind of stood there for a minute, and then I realized I was just standing there grinning like an idiot. Mom was smiling really hard, like she was trying not to laugh. I gave Chris another little wave and almost ran out of the office.

Then Mom took me right to Katie's house, where Katie, Alexis, and Emma were already starting to decorate.

"We get to decorate twenty-five cupcakes each," Alexis informed me. "We saved yours."

She pointed to a tray on Katie's table with an assortment of vanilla, chocolate, and strawberry cupcakes on it. There were bowls of icing and all the decorations we had played around with the week before, plus more.

"This is awesome!" I said, taking a seat. I picked up a bowl of icing that had been dyed blue and started to frost a vanilla cupcake with it. I thought I'd do a sky with fluffy marshmallow clouds.

"Isn't this the best?" Katie asked, making a pattern of colorful candy-coated chocolates on top of a chocolate-iced cupcake. "I think I could make a thousand of these, and they would all be different!"

"Totally," I agreed.

We were so into what we were doing that we didn't talk much, except to show off what we had done. I decorated my cupcakes one by one and then put them in the cupcake carrier. I just had one last little cupcake left, a vanilla one. I spread some vanilla icing on top, looked at it, and then packed it.

"Aren't you going to decorate that one?" Alexis asked.

"I don't think so," I replied. "It's 'Come as You Are,' right? So maybe someone wants to come, you

126

know, plain. Like an almost-naked cupcake."

"But you don't like plain anything!" Katie exclaimed.

"True," I said. "But sometimes plain is all you need. No embellishment required."

Alexis nodded. "Perfect. Now we really have something for everyone."

"And even if it's not perfect, it'll still be good, right?" I teased, thinking about the twins' party.

Alexis smiled. "Of course!"

And I guess that's kind of how I was feeling about myself. I wasn't perfect anymore (and I probably never was to begin with). I had braces. I had glasses. That sure wasn't perfect.

But it was still really good.

CHAPTER 19

Come as You Are

"Wow, it looks really awesome this year!" Katie said.

We had just pulled up to the school in Katie's mom's car. Emma's dad parked next to us in his van. We had a lot of stuff to set up.

The carnival was on the school field, which was filled with colorful booths, tents, and games. As we carried our stuff to our table, we passed a dunk tank with a sign over it that read DUNK THE TEACHER. There was a big board with balloons on it for dart throwing, a cotton candy machine, and a cart selling cold drinks.

"Maybe we can take turns selling cupcakes, so we can all explore the carnival a little bit," Katie said, looking around.

"Let's set up first, and then we can make up a schedule," Alexis suggested.

The school clubs were assigned tables under a big canopy. We found a table with a paper sign with CUPCAKE CLUB written on it and then put our stuff down.

"Oh boy," Alexis said, nodding to the table next to us. "Looks like the BFC are our next-door neighbors." She didn't sound happy.

"I hope they're not doing cupcakes again," Katie said. Once, the BFC had decided to make cupcakes at the fall fund-raiser to compete with us.

"Probably not," Emma guessed. "It didn't work out too well for them last time."

"Come on, let's get everything ready," I urged. I was anxious to see how things were going to look.

We covered the table with a plain white tablecloth, because we wanted a neutral background for our colorful cupcakes. But I had made an equally colorful sign for the front of the table.

A SUMMER OF CUPCAKES
COME AS YOU ARE!
Eat what you want!
The Cupcake Club

I had written the letters in all different colors, and all around the sign I had drawn some of the designs from our cupcakes: rainbows, hearts, stars, smiley faces, sad faces—everything I could think of. It looked really cool when we hung it up.

Then we arranged our one hundred cupcakes in a spiral.

"Awesome!" Alexis said.

"It looks like a crazy kaleidoscope," Katie added.

I took out my phone and then snapped a picture. "We totally did it!"

Alexis began to set up the cash box and calculator, and then Callie, Maggie, Bella, and Olivia walked up to the BFC table. Callie had on her funky glasses, and she looked totally cute.

"Hey," I said. "What are you guys doing?"

Callie put a big plastic tub on the table and then opened the lid. "Friendship bracelets," she said, and I looked inside. The tub was filled with braided friendship bracelets in all different colors and patterns.

"Oh my gosh, that's so cool!" I said. "It must have taken forever to make those."

"Hours and hours," Maggie piped up. "But we're the Best Friends Club, so friendship bracelets are perfect, right?"

Katie walked over. "These are really sweet. You know, our booths kind of go together. You've got all different kinds of friendship bracelets, and we've got all different kinds of cupcakes!"

Olivia rolled her eyes. "That is sooo corny."

I ignored her. "We would look really good wearing friendship bracelets at our booth. How about a trade? Bracelets for cupcakes?"

"What?" Alexis asked, alarmed, looking up from her cash box.

"Come on, Alexis," I said. "We'll still make plenty of money with our other cupcakes. And it's good to support fellow entrepreneurs, right?"

My strategy worked. "All right," Alexis agreed. "Let's trade."

So we looked through the bracelets, and the BFC looked through our cupcakes. Since we were all wearing our Cupcake Club T-shirts, which are mostly pink and yellow, we found bracelets to match.

At our table, Maggie took one of Katie's rainbow cupcakes. Bella found one that Alexis had made with purple icing and black jelly beans. Olivia and Callie picked out ones with edible glitter on top.

"Mmm," Maggie said, biting into her cupcake right away. "Your cupcakes are so good!"

"And these bracelets are awesome," I replied. "Thanks!"

And then people started pouring into the carnival. A lot of people came up to our table and had fun picking out cupcakes. I was busy helping a cute little kid pick out a cupcake when I heard a familiar voice.

"Hey, Mia."

I looked up. It was Chris!

"These cupcakes look good," he said, and as he talked, I could see the metal braces on his teeth. And you know what? He looked just as cute as ever.

"Oh my gosh, you got them!" I exclaimed. "How do you feel?"

"Really sore," he admitted. "I would love a cupcake, but I don't know if I could eat it."

"I have just the one," I said, and I searched the kaleidoscope until I found the almost-naked cupcake I had made. "This one's got no toppings. It's nice and soft and mushy. Sometimes plain vanilla is just what you need."

Chris smiled. "Thanks," he said, fishing in his pocket to pay me. "You're the best."

And then the thing I said next just kind of came out. "So, maybe we could hang out sometime?" I said. "When your braces aren't hurting."

Chris smiled again. "Definitely. I'll text you, okay?"

"Okay."

Chris walked away, and I felt like I was floating on a cloud. It wasn't just because of what happened with Chris. It was because I felt like me again. I looked at the "Come as You Are" cupcakes and smiled. Because from now on I knew I could just be myself and everything would be okay—with four eyes, a mouth full of braces, or even with plain vanilla.

Want another sweet cupcake?
Here's a sneak peek
of the fifteenth book in the
CUPCaKE DIARIES
series:

Emma
sugar and spice
and everything
nice

Poor Jake

Please, Emmy! Just one more lick!"

My younger brother, Jake, was whining at me, which always drives me crazy. I sighed in exasperation.

"Come on, Em, don't be such a tough guy," said my best friend Alexis. Though Jake's the only person I've allowed to call me "Emmy," lately everyone's been calling me "Em," though my full first name is Emma.

"Great, now you're on his side?" I complained.

"I'm always on his side," said Alexis, winking at my little brother.

The Cupcake Club—my best friends, Alexis, Mia, and Katie, plus me—was having a baking session in my kitchen. Whenever we bake at my house, my little brother, Jake, always comes scrounging around for tastes and licks of the batter and frosting, and he's so high maintenance that it drives me crazy.

Jake smiled up at me now with his most winning grin. Alexis put her arm across his shoulders.

"Come on, Em," she said.

"Fine, but he's eating up our profits, you know," I said, trying to appeal to Alexis's astute business sensibility. "Here, at least use a clean spoon. You've had a sore throat."

"I always have a sore throat!" cried Jake, gleefully scooping a big lump of buttercream frosting out of the mixing bowl.

"Strep again?" asked Mia, her brow wrinkling in concern.

I sighed. "Probably."

Jake was right; he does always have a sore throat. And usually an ear infection to go with it. The doctor says Jake's just prone to infections, because of the way his throat and ear canals are built.

I can't think about things like ear canals too much because I get really queasy with body stuff, especially if it comes down to words like "pus," or needles, or most especially, blood (even the word, never mind the sight of it!). Lately, I've even started to faint at the doctor's office and twice, almost, at the dentist's. Most people don't know this about me, because I'm pretty embarrassed about it. It just seems weak and a little babyish, especially at my age. Alexis was at the doctor's office with me once when I had to get a shot and a blood test, so she knows all about it, but no one else really does.

Anyway, I do feel bad for Jake, with all the ear and throat problems, but I am a tiny bit jealous sometimes that he gets to stay home from school so much. Mom makes him soup and pudding, and he watches cartoons in his cozy clothes all day. It looks like heaven, and a sore throat seems like a small price to pay.

Just then my older brother Matt walked in, calling out a hello as he dumped his backpack in his locker in the mudroom. (Yes, we have lockers at home. Kind of pathetic, but my mom says it's the only way to contain the chaos with four busy and athletic kids in the house.) Matt's only a grade ahead of me, so we see each other a lot at school as well as at home, obviously, but Jake doesn't see him that much, so he gets bowled over with excitement when Matt shows up.

"Matty! Come see my drawing I did of the

Miami Heat!" says Jake, dropping his spoon with a clatter into the sink and taking off without even a backward glance.

"Hey! What about us?" asked Mia, who is Jake's special buddy.

But he didn't even hear her.

"The second you arrive, we're dead to him," joked Alexis, who has a crush on Matt. *The same can be said about you, my friend,* I thought, suppressing a giggle.

Matt smiled and shrugged, palms up in the air. "Hey, I can't help it if the kid worships me. Either you've got it or you don't got it, you know?"

"Trust me, you *don't* got it," I said, turning to the sink to start the cleanup.

Jake came tearing back in, a piece of drawing paper flapping in his hands. "Look! Look, Matty, isn't it cool? See that's LeBron, and that's Ray Allen, and here's the basket, and here's you and me in the stands. . . ."

Matt glanced down at it. "Sweet," he said, barely standing still for even a second. He passed by Jake and went to get a glass from the cabinet and poured himself some juice. Jake stood still in the middle of the kitchen, unsure of whether or not to follow Matt.

"Hey, can I see it, Jake?" asked Katie, swooping in to mask Matt's lack of enthusiasm. She reached for the drawing, but Jake snatched it away.

"No! It's just for boys! It's basketball!" said Jake, all snotty.

"Jake! That's rude!" I cried. "Katie's just trying to—" I caught myself before I said "make you feel better." Phew. "Um, see how far your drawing's come this semester," I finished lamely.

"No," said Jake. "Matty, what are you doing now?"

There was a pause as Matt finished gulping down his juice. "Homework," he said, clearing his throat and giving a huge burp.

All the girls groaned, but Jake giggled gleefully. "Good one!" Jake said.

"OMG, he even worships your burps," I said. "Pathetic."

Matt smiled and shrugged again. Then he reached out and tousled Jake's hair. "See ya later, little buddy." He grabbed his backpack from the mudroom and then went upstairs.

Jake sat down in a kitchen chair, his drawing hanging limply at his side. He put his forehead in his hand, like he always does when he's thinking really hard.

"Want to draw with me?" asked Mia, who's very

artistic. Jake loves drawing with her. She's so good, she can draw anything and have it look like what it's supposed to, unlike me. Everything I draw ends up looking like a chicken.

Jake shook his head.

"What are you thinking about?" asked Katie, all perky and trying to cheer up Jake.

He looked at her and then kind of snapped out of his trance. "How I can draw better so Matty will like it."

We all looked at one another in pain. The poor kid. He so looks up to Matt and our oldest brother, Sam, but they are just too busy for him. I'm the one who spends time with him, but he couldn't care less about me, unless I have something sugary he wants to eat.

"Jake, you're a great artist!" Mia declared.

"Not that much," said Jake. He put his drawing on the kitchen table. "I'm going to watch TV," he said, and left the room.

"Okay, my heart is officially broken," said Mia once he was out of earshot.

"I know. It's sad," I agreed. "But he *is* high maintenance, and after a while it gets old."

"It would never get old for me," said Katie, who's an only child.

"Me neither," agreed Mia, who has only her older stepbrother, Dan.

I sighed heavily and sat down at the table, drying my hands on a dishtowel.

"I get it," said Alexis. "I still think it's sad, but I do get how Emma feels."

I alternated between feeling very sympathetic toward Jake or very frustrated with him, sometimes within seconds. Like now.

"Okay, enough about Jake," I said. "Let's talk about what jobs we have lined up for the Cupcake Club."

We all sat at the table, and Alexis, who is our CEO, took out her laptop and began our meeting.

"Let's see, we have Mallory Clifford's birthday party this weekend. Three dozen Mud Pies. Plus Mona tomorrow . . ."

Mona is one of our regular customers. She owns The Special Day bridal salon and has a standing order for four dozen all-white mini cupcakes each Saturday. They're for her brides to eat, so they don't get all hungry and cranky while they're trying on dresses.

"Any modeling jobs coming up for you?" asked Katie.

I shook my head. I've done a bunch of modeling

this year for Mona—mostly trunk shows, where I walk around in sample junior bridesmaid dresses—but also a little bit of print work, which is really just another word for a newspaper or magazine ad. I got started doing a print ad for Mona, and other clients saw it. "There's not much this month. It's kind of the off-season for trunk shows," I said. Even though I was kind of happy for the break (modeling is hard work, believe it or not), I could use some money. A little job would be okay right about now, especially some print work. The cash is good.

"Focus, people, and we can wrap this up," said Alexis, who is all about being an efficient manager.

"Oh, one of my mom's friends from work wants us to do a dessert for the book club she's hosting. My mom is going to it too," said Mia. "I'll follow up on that." She punched a reminder into her phone.

"Good," said Alexis. "We could use some more business and some new clients. We need to branch out."

"Hey, don't forget we have that bachelorette party for Mona's client in two Saturdays," I said.

"Yup. Got it right here," said Alexis, looking at her calendar. "Three dozen. Our choice of flavor."

While we were reviewing the order, my mom walked in. "Hello, Cupcakers!" she greeted cheerily. My mom loves my friends, which gives me such a happy and cozy feeling.

"Hi, Mrs. Taylor!" they all replied. They love her, too.

"What's up?" asked Alexis. My mom doesn't usually get home from work until five fifteen, and it was only four thirty now.

My mom grimaced. "I'm only here for a second. I have to take Jake to the doctor again. *They're talking about taking out his tonsils.*" She whispered the last part.

"Bummer," said Alexis.

"Dan had that done. It really hurts," whispered Mia.

"I know. But it's a pretty routine outpatient operation, and I guess the long-term payoff is worth it," said my mom.

"Definitely," Mia agreed, nodding. "Dan hasn't had a sore throat since."

"Well, here goes," said my mom. Then she called out, "Jake! Hi, honey! Time for the doctor!" and left the room in search of my little brother.

"I didn't want to say anything in front of your mom to worry her, but," said Mia quietly, "Dan couldn't eat anything but soft food for almost two weeks."

"Wow. Maybe we'll have to make Jake big bowls of frosting to fatten him up!" said Alexis.

"You're making me frosting?" asked Jake, walking into the room and shrugging on his hoodie.

"Maybe!" said Alexis, with a twinkle in her eye.

"I'll be good! I promise!" said Jake.

Mia grabbed him in a playful hug. "You're always good! It has nothing to do with that!" she said, tickling him.

He laughed and shrieked, and she let him go.

"Bye, big guy!" called Mia.

He waved and followed my mom out the door.

"He doesn't even know what's coming," said Katie mournfully.

"It's just tonsils!" I said, swatting her with the dishtowel. "He's not having heart surgery!"

But I knew Jake would not be psyched. It might as well be heart surgery. And deep down inside, I worried for him just the same.

Coco Simon always dreamed of opening a cupcake bakery but was afraid she would eat all of the profits. When she's not daydreaming about cupcakes, Coco edits children's books and has written close to one hundred books for children, tweens, and young adults, which is a lot less than the number of cupcakes she's eaten. Cupcake Diaries is the first time Coco has mixed her love of cupcakes with writing.

Mia's Missing Glasses

Oh no! Not today, Mia thought.

"Help!" Mia cried to all her Cupcake friends.

Emma turned and asked her what was wrong.

"Right now I have about five minutes to get to my big math test, and I can't find my glasses," Mia said sadly.

"Ha!" Katie said and nudged Emma and Alexis.

Emma started cracking up next. Alexis started laughing too!

"Don't worry, Mia, because we know exactly where your glasses are," Katie said with a grin.

Where were Mia's glasses?

Circle the first letter of each sentence, and write it below on the lines. (If you don't want to write in your book, make a copy of this page.)

They were _ _ _ _ _ _ _ _ _ !

A Recipe for Disaster!

Mia was thinking about her new crush, Chris, when she should have been writing down ingredients for a new cupcake recipe. When she looked down at her page, she realized she had scrambled all the ingredients! Can you help Mia and unscramble each word? Write each word correctly on the lines. Then write the circled letters in order on the lines at the bottom of the page.

You'll find out something that happens in our next Cupcake Diaries book, *Emma Sugar and Spice and Everything Nice*.

(If you don't want to write in your book, make a copy of this page.)

1. UTNOCCO _ _ _ _ _ _ ⊙
2. MLAONDS _ _ _ ⊙ _ _ _
3. METNUG ⊙ _ _ _ _ _
4. TASL ⊙ _ _ _
5. KILM _ ⊙ _ _
6. MONLE ⊙ _ _ _ _
7. HOLACTECO _ _ _ _ _ ⊙ _ _ _
8. NTMI _ _ ⊙ _
9. TRADUCS _ _ _ ⊙ _ _ _
10. NILAVLA _ _ _ ⊙ _ _ _
11. SELKNIRPS ⊙ _ _ _ _ _ _ _ _

In *Emma, Sugar and Spice and Everything Nice*,

Jake gets _ _ _ _ _ _ _ _ _ _ _ !

All Eyes on Mia!

In this story, at first Mia is worried that she has to wear glasses.
But by the end of the book, Mia realizes that wearing glasses is not only
not such a big deal, they can be awesome fashion accessories too!
What kind of glasses do you think Mia should wear?
Draw them here on Mia.

(If you don't want to write in your book, make a copy of this page.)

Answer Key

Mia's Missing Glasses

Oh no! **N**ot today, Mia thought.

"**H**elp!" Mia cried to all her Cupcake friends.

Emma turned and asked her what was wrong.

"**R**ight now I have about five minutes to get to my big math test, and I can't find my glasses," Mia said sadly.

"**H**a!" Katie said and nudged Emma and Alexis.

Emma started cracking up next. **A**lexis started laughing too!

"**D**on't worry, Mia, because we know exactly where your glasses are," Katie said with a grin.

Where were Mia's glasses?
They were ON HER HEAD!

A Recipe for Disaster!

COCONUT, ALMONDS, NUTMEG, SALT, MILK, LEMON,
CHOCOLATE, MINT, CUSTARD, VANILLA, SPRINKLES
Jake gets TONSILLITIS!

Still Hungry?

There's always room for another Cupcake!

Katie and the Cupcake Cure

978-1-4424-2275-9 $5.99
978-1-4424-2276-6 (eBook)

Mia in the Mix

978-1-4424-2277-3 $5.99
978-1-4424-2278-0 (eBook)

Emma on Thin Icing

978-1-4424-2279-7 $5.99
978-1-4424-2280-3 (eBook)

Alexis and the Perfect Recipe

978-1-4424-2901-7 $5.99
978-1-4424-2902-4 (eBook)

Katie, Batter Up!

978-1-4424-4611-3 $5.99
978-1-4424-4612-0 (eBook)

Mia's Baker's Dozen

978-1-4424-4613-7 $5.99
978-1-4424-4614-4 (eBook)

Emma All Stirred Up!

978-1-4424-5078-3 $5.99
978-1-4424-5079-0 (eBook)

Alexis Cool as a Cupcake

978-1-4424-5080-6 $5.99
978-1-4424-5081-3 (eBook)

Katie and the Cupcake War

978-1-4424-5373-9 $5.99
978-1-4424-5374-6 (eBook)

Mia's Boiling Point

978-1-4424-5396-8 $5.99
978-1-4424-5397-5 (eBook)

Emma, Smile and Say "Cupcake!"

978-1-4424-5398-2 $5.99
978-1-4424-5400-2 (eBook)

Alexis Gets Frosted

978-1-4424-6867-2 $5.99
978-1-4424-6868-9 (eBook)

Katie's New Recipe

978-1-4424-7168-9 $5.99
978-1-4424-7169-6 (eBook)

Mia a Matter of Taste

978-1-4424-7435-2 $5.99
978-1-4424-7436-9 (eBook)

Emma Sugar and Spice and Everything Nice

978-1-4424-7488-8 $5.99
978-1-4424-7489-5 (eBook)